Cyrus Adler

Allan Ramsay

Turkish Coffee House Tales

EUROPÄISCHER
HOCH
SCHUL
VERLAG

Adler, Cyrus

Ramsay, Allan

Turkish Coffee House Tales

ISBN/EAN: 978-3-86741-440-1
First published in 2010 by Europaeischer Hochschulverlag
GmbH & Co KG, Bremen, Germany.

Cyrus Adler

Allan Ramsay

Turkish Coffee House Tales

EUROPÄISCHER
HOCH
SCHUL
VERLAG

PREFACE

In the course of a number of visits to Constantinople, I became much interested in the tales that are told in the coffee houses. These are usually little more than rooms, with walls made of small panes of glass. The furniture consists of a tripod with a contrivance for holding the kettle, and a fire to keep the coffee boiling. A carpeted bench traverses the entire length of the room. This is occupied by turbaned Turks, their legs folded under them, smoking nargilehs or chibooks or cigarettes, and sipping coffee. A few will be engaged in a game of backgammon, but the majority enter into conversation, at first only in syllables, which gradually gives rise to a general discussion. Finally, some sage of the neighborhood comes in, and the company appeals to him to settle the point at issue. This he usually does by telling a story to illustrate his opinion. Some of the stories told on these occasions are adaptations of those already known in Arabic and Persian literature, but the Turkish mind gives them a new setting and a peculiar philosophy. They are characteristic of the habits, customs, and methods of thought of the people, and for this reason seem worthy of preservation.

Two of these tales have been taken from the Armenian, and were received from Dr. K. Ohannassian of Constantinople. For one, *The Merciful Khan*, I am indebted to Mr. George Kennan. None of them has been translated from any book or manuscript, and all are, as nearly as practicable, in the form in which they are usually narrated. Most of the stories have been collected by Mr. Allan Ramsay, who, by a long residence in Constantinople, has had special opportunities for learning to know the modern Turk. It is due to him, however, to say that for the style and editing he is in no wise responsible, and that all sins of omission and commission must be laid at my door.

CYRUS ADLER.

Cosmos Club, Washington,
February 1, 1898.

CONTENTS

HOW THE HODJA SAVED ALLAH

Not far from the famous Mosque Bayezid an old Hodja kept a school, and very skilfully he taught the rising generation the everlasting lesson from the Book of Books. Such knowledge had he of human nature that by a glance at his pupil he could at once tell how long it would take him to learn a quarter of the Koran. He was known over the whole Empire as the best reciter and imparter of the Sacred Writings of the Prophet. For many years this Hodja, famed far and wide as the Hodja of Hodjas, had taught in this little school. The number of times he had recited the Book with his pupils is beyond counting; and should we attempt to consider how often he must have corrected them for some misplaced word, our beards would grow gray in the endeavor.

Swaying to and fro one day as fast as his old age would let him, and reciting to his pupils the latter part of one of the chapters, Bakara, divine inspiration opened his inward eye and led him to pause at the following sentence: "And he that spends his money in the ways of Allah is likened unto a grain of wheat that brings forth seven sheaves, and in each sheaf an hundred grains; and Allah giveth twofold unto whom He pleaseth." As his pupils, one after the other, recited this verse to him, he wondered why he had overlooked its meaning for so many years. Fully convinced that anything either given to Allah, or in the way that He proposes, was an investment that brought a percentage undreamed of in known commerce, he dismissed his pupils, and putting his hand into his bosom drew forth from the many folds of his dress a bag, and proceeded to count his worldly possessions.

Carefully and attentively he counted and then recounted his money, and found that if invested in the ways of Allah it would bring a return of no less than one thousand piasters.

"Think of it," said the Hodja to himself, "one thousand piasters! One thousand piasters! Mashallah! a fortune."

So, having dismissed his school, he sallied forth, his bag of money in his hand, and began distributing its contents to the needy that he met in the highways. Ere many hours had passed the whole of his savings was gone. The Hodja was very happy; for now he was the creditor in Allah's books for one thousand piasters.

He returned to his house and ate his evening meal of bread and olives, and was content.

The next day came. The thousand piasters had not yet arrived. He ate his bread, he imagined he had olives, and was content.

The third day came. The old Hodja had no bread and he had no olives. He suffered the pangs of hunger. So when the end of the day had come, and his pupils had departed to their homes, the Hodja, with a full heart and an empty stomach, walked out of the town, and soon got beyond the city walls.

There, where no one could hear him, he lamented his sad fate, and the great calamity that had befallen him in his old age.

What sin had he committed? What great wrong had his ancestors done, that the wrath of the Almighty had thus fallen on him, when his earthly course was well-nigh run?

"Ya! Allah! Allah!" he cried, and beat his breast.

As if in answer to his cry, the howl of the dreaded Fakir Dervish came over across the plain. In those days the Fakir Dervish was a terror in the land. He knocked at the door, and it was opened. He asked, and received food. If refused, life often paid the penalty.

The Hodja's lamentations were now greater than ever; for should the Dervish ask him for food and the Hodja have nothing to give, he would certainly be killed.

"Allah! Allah! Allah! Guide me now. Protect one of your faithful followers," cried the frightened Hodja, and he looked around to see if there was any one to rescue him from his perilous position. But not a soul was to be seen, and the walls of the city were five miles distant. Just then the howl of the Dervish again reached his ear, and in terror he flew, he knew not whither. As luck would have it he came upon a tree, up which, although stiff from age and weak from want, the Hodja, with wonderful agility, scrambled and, trembling like a leaf, awaited his fate.

Nearer and nearer came the howling Dervish, till at last his long hair could be seen floating in the air, as with rapid strides he preceded the wind upon his endless journey.

On and on he came, his wild yell sending the blood, from very fear, to unknown parts of the poor Hodja's body and leaving his face as yellow as a melon.

To his utter dismay, the Hodja saw the Dervish

approach the tree and sit down under its shade.

Sighing deeply, the Dervish said in a loud voice, "Why have I come into this world? Why were my forefathers born? Why was anybody born? Oh, Allah! Oh, Allah! What have you done! Misery! Misery! Nothing but misery to mankind and everything living. Shall I not be avenged for all the misery my father and my father's fathers have suffered? I shall be avenged."

Striking his chest a loud blow, as if to emphasize the decision he had come to, the Dervish took a small bag that lay by his side, and slowly proceeded to untie the leather strings that bound it. Bringing forth from it a small image, he gazed at it a moment and then addressed it in the following terms:

"You, Job! you bore much; you have written a book in which your history is recorded; you have earned the reputation of being the most patient man that ever lived; yet I have read your history and found that when real affliction oppressed you, you cursed God. You have made men believe, too, that there is a reward in this life for all the afflictions they suffer. You have misled mankind. For these sins no one has ever punished you. Now I will punish you," and taking his long, curved sword in his hand he cut off the head of the figure.

The Dervish bent forward, took another image and, gazing upon it with a contemptuous smile, thus addressed it:

"David, David, singer of songs of peace in this world and in the world to come, I have read your sayings in which you counsel men to lead a righteous life for the sake of the reward which they are to receive. I have learned that you have misled your fellow-mortals with your songs of peace and joy. I have read your history, and I find that you have committed many sins. For these sins and for misleading your fellowmen you have never been punished. Now I will punish you," and taking his sword in his hand he cut off David's head.

Again the Dervish bent forward and brought forth an image which he addressed as follows:

"You, Solomon, are reputed to have been the wisest man that ever lived. You had command over the host of the Genii and could control the legion of the demons. They came at the bidding of your signet ring, and they trembled at the mysterious names to which you gave utterance. You understood every living thing. The speech of the beasts of the field, of the birds of the air, of the insects of the earth, and of the fishes of the sea, was known unto you. Yet when I read your history I found that in spite of the vast knowledge that was vouchsafed unto you, you committed many wrongs and did many foolish things, which in the end brought misery into the world and destruction unto your people; and for all these no one has ever punished you. Now I will punish you," and taking his sword he cut off Solomon's head.

Again the Dervish bent forward and brought forth from the bag another figure, which he addressed thus:

"Jesus, Jesus, prophet of God, you came into this world to atone, by giving your blood, for the sins of mankind and to bring unto them a religion of peace. You founded a church, whose history I have studied, and I see that it set fathers against their children and brethren against one another; that it brought strife into the world; that the lives of men and women and children were sacrificed so that the rivers ran red with blood unto the seas. Truly you were a great prophet, but the misery you caused must be avenged. For it no one has yet punished you. Now I will punish you," and he took his sword and cut off Jesus' head.

With a sorrowful face the Dervish bent forward and brought forth another image from the bag.

"Mohammed," he said, "I have slain Job, David, Solomon, and Jesus. What shall I do with you? After the followers of Jesus had shed much blood, their religion spread over the world, was acceptable unto man, and the nations were at peace. Then you came into the world, and you brought a new religion, and father rose against father, and brother rose against brother; hatred was sown between your followers and the followers of Jesus, and again the rivers ran red with blood unto the seas; and you have not been punished. For this I will punish you. By the beard of my forefathers, whose blood was made to flow in your cause, you too must die," and with a blow the head of Mohammed fell to the ground.

Then the Dervish prostrated himself to the earth, and after a silent prayer rose and brought forth from the bag the last figure. Reverently he bowed to it, and then he addressed it as follows:

"Oh, Allah! The Allah of Allahs. There is but one Allah, and thou art He. I have slain Job, David, Solomon, Jesus, and Mohammed for the folly that they have brought into the world. Thou, God, art all powerful. All men are thy children, thou createst them and bringest them into the world. The thoughts that they think are thy thoughts. If all these men have brought all this evil into the world, it is thy fault. Shall I punish them and allow thee to go unhurt? No. I must punish thee also," and he raised his sword to strike.

As the sword circled in the air the Hodja, secreted in the tree, forgot the fear in which he stood of the Dervish. In the excitement of the moment he cried out in a loud tone of voice: "Stop! Stop! He owes me one thousand piasters."

The Dervish reeled and fell senseless to the ground. The Hodja was overcome at his own words and trembled with fear, convinced that his last hour had arrived. The Dervish lay stretched upon his back on the grass like one dead. At last the Hodja took courage. Breaking a twig from off the tree, he threw it down upon the Dervish's face, but the Dervish made no sign. The Hodja took more courage, removed one of his heavy outer shoes and threw it on the outstretched figure of the Dervish, but still the Dervish lay motionless. The Hodja carefully climbed down the tree, gave the body of the Dervish a kick, and climbed back again, and still the Dervish did not stir. At length the Hodja descended from the tree and placed his ear to the Dervish's heart. It did not beat. The Dervish was dead.

"Ah, well," said the Hodja, "at least I shall not starve. I will take his garments and sell them and buy me some bread."

The Hodja commenced to remove the Dervish's garments. As he took off his belt he found that it was heavy. He opened it, and saw that it contained gold. He counted the gold and found that it was exactly one thousand piasters.

The Hodja turned his face toward Mecca and raising his eyes to heaven said, "Oh God, you have kept your promise, but," he added, "not before I saved your life."

BETTER IS THE FOLLY OF WOMAN
THAN THE WISDOM OF MAN

There lived in Constantinople an old Hodja, a learned man, who had a son. The boy followed in his father's footsteps, went every day to the Mosque Aya Sofia, seated himself in a secluded spot, to the left of the pillar bearing the impress of the Conqueror's hand, and engaged in the study of the Koran. Daily he might be seen seated, swaying his body to and fro, and reciting to himself the verses of the Holy Book.

The dearest wish of a Mohammedan theological student is to be able to recite the entire Koran by heart. Many years are spent in memorizing the Holy Book, which must be recited with a prescribed cantillation, and in acquiring a rhythmical movement of the body which accompanies the chant.

When Abdul, for that was the young man's name, had reached his nineteenth year, he had, by the most assiduous study, finally succeeded in mastering three-fourths of the Koran. At this achievement his pride rose, his ambition was fired, and he determined to become a great man.

The day that he reached this decision he did not go to the Mosque, but stopped at home, in his father's house, and sat staring at the fire burning in the grate. Several times the father asked:

"My son, what do you see in the fire?"

And each time the son answered:

"Nothing, father."

He was very young; he could not see.

Finally, the young man picked up courage and gave expression to his thoughts.

"Father," he said, "I wish to become a great man."

"That is very easy," said the father.

"And to be a great man," continued the son, "I must first go to Mecca." For no Mohammedan priest or theologian, or even layman, has fulfilled all of the cardinal precepts of his faith unless he has made the pilgrimage to the Holy City.

To his son's last observation the father blandly replied: "It is very easy to go to Mecca."

"How, easy?" asked the son. "On the contrary, it is very difficult; for the journey is costly, and I have no money."

"Listen, my son," said the father. "You must become a scribe, the writer of the thoughts of your brethren, and your fortune is made."

"But I have not even the implements necessary for a scribe," said the son.

"All that can be easily arranged," said the father; "your grandfather had an ink-horn; I will give it you; I will buy you some writing-paper, and we will get you a box to sit in; all that you need to do is to sit still, look wise and your fortune is made."

And indeed the advice was good. For letter-writing is an art which only the few possess. The ability to write by no means carries with it the ability to compose. Epistolary genius is rare.

Abdul was much rejoiced at the counsel that had been given him, and lost no time in carrying out the plan. He took his grandfather's ink-horn, the paper his father bought, got himself a box and began his career as a scribe.

Abdul was a child, he knew nothing, but deeming himself wise he sought to surpass the counsel of his father.

"To look wise," he said, "is not sufficient; I must have some other attraction."

And after much thought he hit upon the following idea. Over his box he painted a legend: "The wisdom of man is greater than the wisdom of woman." People thought the sign very clever, customers came, the young Hodja took in many piasters and he was correspondingly happy.

This sign one day attracted the eyes and mind of a Hanoum (Turkish lady). Seeing that Abdul was a manly youth, she went to him and said:

"Hodja, I have a difficult letter to write. I have heard that thou art very wise, so I have come to thee. To write the letter thou wilt need all thy wit. Moreover, the letter is a long one, and I cannot stand here while it is being written. Come to my Konak (house) at three this afternoon, and we will write the letter."

The Hodja was overcome with admiration for his fair client, and surprised at the invitation. He was enchanted, his heart beat wildly, and so great was his agitation that his reply of acquiescence was scarcely audible.

The invitation had more than the charm of novelty to make it attractive. He had never talked with a woman outside of his own family circle. To be admitted to a lady's house was in itself an adventure.

Long before the appointed time, the young Hodja — impetuous youth — gathered together his reeds, ink, and sand. With feverish step he wended his way to the house. Lattices covered the windows, a high wall surrounded the garden, and a ponderous gate barred the entrance. Thrice he raised the massive knocker.

"Who is there?" called a voice from within.

"The scribe," was the reply.

"It is well," said the porter; the gate was unbarred, and the Hodja permitted to enter. Directly he was ushered into the apartment of his fair client.

The lady welcomed him cordially.

"Ah! Hodja Effendi, I am glad to see you; pray sit down."

The Hodja nervously pulled out his writing-implements.

"Do not be in such a hurry," said the lady. "Refresh yourself; take a cup of coffee, smoke a cigarette, and we will write the letter afterwards."

So he lit a cigarette, drank a cup of coffee, and they fell to talking. Time flew; the minutes seemed like seconds, and the hours were as minutes. While they were thus enjoying themselves there suddenly came a heavy knock at the gate.

"It is my husband, the Pasha," cried the lady. "What shall I do? If he finds you here, he will kill you! I am so frightened."

The Hodja was frightened too. Again there came a knock at the gate.

"I have it," and taking Abdul by the arm, she

said, "you must get into the box," indicating a large chest in the room. "Quick, quick, if you prize your life utter not a word, and Inshallah I will save you."

Abdul now, too late, saw his folly. It was his want of experience; but driven by the sense of danger, he entered the chest; the lady locked it and took the key.

A moment afterwards the Pasha came in.

"I am very tired," he said; "bring me coffee and a chibook."

"Good evening, Pasha Effendi," said the lady. "Sit down. I have something to tell you."

"Bah!" said the Pasha; "I want none of your woman's talk; 'the hair of woman is long, and her wits are short,' says the proverb. Bring me my pipe."

"But, Pasha Effendi," said the lady, "I have had an adventure to-day."

"Bah!" said the Pasha; "what adventure can a woman have — forgot to paint your eyebrows or color your nails, I suppose."

"No, Pasha Effendi. Be patient, and I will tell you. I went out to-day to write a letter."

"A letter?" said the Pasha; "to whom would you write a letter?"

"Be patient," she said, "and I will tell you my story. So I came to the box of a young scribe with beautiful eyes."

"A young man with beautiful eyes," shouted the Pasha. "Where is he? I'll kill him!" and he drew his sword.

The Hodja in the chest heard every word and

trembled in every limb.

"Be patient, Pasha Effendi; I said I had an adventure, and you did not believe me. I told the young man that the letter was long, and I could not stand in the street to write it. So I asked him to come and see me this afternoon."

"Here? to this house?" thundered the Pasha.

"Yes, Pasha Effendi," said the lady. "So the Hodja came here, and I gave him coffee and a cigarette, and we talked, and the minutes seemed like seconds, and the hours were as minutes. All at once came your knock at the gate, and I said to the Hodja, 'That is the Pasha; and if he finds you here, he will kill you.'"

"And I will kill him," screamed the Pasha, "where is he?"

"Be patient, Pasha Effendi," said the lady, "and I will tell you. When you knocked a second time, I suddenly thought of the chest, and I put the Hodja in."

"Let me at him!" screamed the Pasha. "I'll cut off his head!"

"O Pasha," she said, "what a hurry you are in to slay this comely youth. He is your prey; he cannot escape you. The youth is not only in the box, but it is locked, and the key is in my pocket. Here it is."

The lady walked over to the Pasha, stretched out her hand and gave him the key.

As he took it, she said:

"Philopena!"

"Bah!" said the Pasha, in disgust. He threw the

key on the floor and left the harem, slamming the door behind him.

After he had gone, the lady took up the key, unlocked the door, and let out the trembling Hodja.

"Go now, Hodja, to your box," she said. "Take down your sign and write instead: 'The wit of woman is twofold the wit of man,' for I am a woman, and in one day I have fooled two men."

THE HANOUM AND THE UNJUST CADI

t was, and still is, in some parts of Constantinople, the custom of the refuse-gatherer to go about the streets with a basket on his back, and a wooden shovel in his hand, calling out 'refuse removed.'

A certain Chepdji, plying his trade, had, in the course of five years of assiduous labor, amassed, to him, the no unimportant sum of five hundred piasters. He was afraid to keep this money by him; so hearing the Cadi of Stamboul highly and reverently spoken of, he decided to entrust his hard-earned savings to the Cadi's keeping.

Going to the Cadi, he said: "Oh learned and righteous man, for five long years have I labored, carrying the dregs and dross of rich and poor alike, and I have saved a sum of five hundred piasters. With the help of Allah, in another two years I shall have saved a further sum of at least one hundred piasters, when, Inshallah, I shall return to my country and clasp my wife and children again. In the meantime you will be granting a boon to your slave, if you will consent to keep this money for me until the time for departure has come."

The Cadi replied: "Thou hast done well, my son; the money will be kept and given to thee when required."

The poor Chepdji, well satisfied, departed. But after a very short time he learned that several of his friends were about to return to their Memleket (province), and he decided to join them, thinking that his five hundred piasters were ample for the time being, 'Besides,' said he, 'who knows what may or may not happen in the next two years?' So he decided to depart with his friends at once.

He went to the Cadi, explained that he had changed his mind, that he was going to leave for his country immediately, and asked for his money. The Cadi called him a dog and ordered him to be whipped out of the place by his servants. Alas! what could the poor Chepdji do! He wept in impotent despair, as he counted the number of years he must yet work before beholding his loved ones.

One day, while moving the dirt from the Konak of a wealthy Pasha, his soul uttered a sigh which reached the ears of the Hanoum, and from the window she asked him why he sighed so deeply. He replied that he sighed for something that could in no way interest her. The Hanoum's sympathy was excited, and after much persuasion, he finally, with tears in his eyes, related to her his great misfortune. The Hanoum thought for a few minutes and then told him to go the following day to the Cadi at a certain hour and again ask for the money as if nothing had happened.

The Hanoum in the meantime gathered together a quantity of jewelry, to the value of several hundred pounds, and instructed her favorite and confidential slave to come with her to the Cadi and remain outside whilst she went in, directing her that when she saw the Chepdji come out and learned that he had gotten his money, to come in the Cadi's room hurriedly and say to her, "your husband has arrived from Egypt, and is waiting for you at the Konak."

The Hanoum then went to the Cadi, carrying in

her hand a bag containing the jewelry. With a profound salaam she said:

"Oh Cadi, my husband, who is in Egypt and who has been there for several years, has at last asked me to come and join him there; these jewels are of great value, and I hesitate to take them with me on so long and dangerous a journey. If you would kindly consent to keep them for me until my return, or if I never return to keep them as a token of my esteem, I will think of you with lifelong gratitude."

The Hanoum then began displaying the rich jewelry. Just then the Chepdji entered, and bending low, said:

"Oh master, your slave has come for his savings in order to proceed to his country."

"Ah, welcome," said the Cadi, "so you are going already!" and immediately ordered the treasurer to pay the five hundred piasters to the Chepdji.

"You see," said the Cadi to the Hanoum, "what confidence the people have in me. This money I have held for some time without receipt or acknowledgment; but directly it is asked for it is paid."

No sooner had the Chepdji gone out of the door, than the Hanoum's slave came rushing in, crying: "Hanoum Effendi! Hanoum Effendi! Your husband has arrived from Egypt, and is anxiously awaiting you at the Konak."

The Hanoum, in well-feigned excitement, gathered up her jewelry and, wishing the Cadi a thousand years of happiness, departed.

The Cadi was thunderstruck, and caressing his beard with grave affection thoughtfully said: "Allah!

Allah! For forty years have I been judge, but never was a cause pleaded in this fashion before."

WHAT HAPPENED TO HADJI, A MER-CHANT OF THE BEZESTAN

Hadji was a married man, but even Turkish married men are not invulnerable to the charms of other women. It happened one day, when possibly the engrossing power of his lawful wife's influence was feeble upon him, that a charming Hanoum came to his shop to purchase some spices. After the departure of his fair visitor Hadji, do what he might, could not drive from his mind's eye, either her image, or her attractive power. He was further greatly puzzled by a tiny black bag containing twelve grains of wheat, which the Hanoum had evidently forgotten.

Till a late hour that night did Hadji remain in his shop, in the hope that either the Hanoum or one of her servants would come for the bag, and thus give him the means of seeing her again or at least of learning where she lived. But Hadji was doomed to disappointment, and, much preoccupied, he returned to his home. There he sat, unresponsive to his wife's conversation, thinking, and no doubt making mental comparisons between her and his visitor.

Hadji remained downcast day after day, and at last, giving way to his wife's entreaties to share his troubles, he frankly told her what had happened, and that ever since that day his soul was in his visitor's bondage.

"Oh husband," replied his wife, "and do you not understand what that black bag containing the twelve grains of wheat means?"

"Alas! no," replied Hadji.

"Why, my husband, it is plain, plain as if it had been told. She lives in the Wheat Market, at house No. 12, with a black door."

Much excited, Hadji rushed off and found that there was a No. 12 in the Wheat Market, with a black door, so he promptly knocked. The door opened, and who should he behold but the lady in question? She, however, instead of speaking to him, threw a basin of water out into the street and then shut the door. Hadji, with mingled feelings of gratitude to his wife for having so accurately directed him, but none the less surprised at his reception, lingered about the doorway for a time and then returned home. He greeted his wife more pleasantly than he had for many days, and told her of his strange reception.

"Why," said his wife, "don't you understand what the basin of water thrown out of the door means?"

"Alas! no," said Hadji.

"Veyh! Veyh! (an exclamation of pity) it means that at the back of the house there is a running stream, and that you must go to her that way."

Off rushed Hadji and found that his wife was right; there was a running stream at the back of the house, so he knocked at the back door. The Hanoum, however, instead of opening it, came to the window, showed a mirror, reversed it and then disappeared. Hadji lingered at the back of the house for a long time, but seeing no further sign of life, he returned to his home much dejected. On entering the house, his wife greeted him with: "Well, was it not as I told you?"

"Yes," said Hadji. "You are truly a wonderful woman, Mashallah! But I do not know why she came to the window and showed me a mirror both in front and back, instead of opening the door."

"Oh," said his wife, "that is very simple; she means that you must go when the face of the moon has reversed itself, about ten o'clock." The hour arrived, Hadji hurried off, and so did his wife; the one to see his love, and the other to inform the police.

Whilst Hadji and his charmer were talking in the garden the police seized them and carried them both off to prison, and Hadji's wife, having accomplished her mission, returned home.

The next morning she baked a quantity of lokum cakes, and taking them to the prison, begged entrance of the guards and permission to distribute these cakes to the prisoners, for the repose of the souls of her dead. This being a request which could not be denied, she was allowed to enter. Finding the cell in which the lady who had infatuated her husband was confined, she offered to save her the disgrace of the exposure, provided she would consent never again to look upon Hadji, the merchant, with envious or loving eyes. The conditions were gratefully accepted, and Hadji's wife changed places with the prisoner.

When they were brought before the judge, Hadji was thunderstruck to see his wife, but being a wise man he held his peace, and left her to do the talking, which she did most vigorously, vehemently protesting against the insult inflicted on both her and her husband in bringing them to prison, because they chose to converse in a garden, being lawfully wedded people; in witness whereof, she called upon the Bekdji (watchman) and the Imam (priest) of the district and several of her neighbors.

Poor Hadji was dumfounded, and, accompanied by his better half, left the prison, where he had expected to stay at least a year or two, saying: "Truly thou art a wonderful woman, Mashallah."

HOW THE JUNKMAN TRAVELLED TO FIND TREASURE IN HIS OWN YARD

In one of the towers overlooking the Sea of Marmora and skirting the ancient city of Stamboul, there lived an old junkman, who earned a precarious livelihood in gathering cinders and useless pieces of iron, and selling them to smiths.

Often did he moralize on the sad Kismet that had reduced him to the task of daily laboring for his bread to make a shoe, perhaps for an ass. Surely he, a true Mussulman, might at least be permitted to ride the ass. His eternal longing often found satisfaction in passing his hours of sleep in dreams of wealth and luxury. But with the dawning of the day came reality and increased longing.

Often did he call on the spirit of sleep to reverse matters, but in vain; with the rising of the sun began the gathering of the cinders and iron.

One night he dreamt that he begged this nocturnal visitor to change his night to day, and the spirit said to him: "Go to Egypt, and it shall be so."

This encouraging phrase haunted him by day and inspired him by night. So persecuted was he with the thought that when his wife said to him, from the door, "Have you brought home any bread?" he would reply, "No, I have not gone; I will go to-morrow;" thinking she had asked him, "Have you gone to Egypt?"

At last, when friends and neighbors began to pity poor Ahmet, for that was his name, as a man on whom the hand of Allah was heavily laid, removing his intelligence, he one morning left his house, saying: "I go! I go! to the land of wealth!" And he left his wife wringing her hands in despair, while the neighbors tried to comfort her. Poor Ahmet went straight on board a boat which he had been told was bound for Iskender (Alexandria), and assured the captain that he was summoned thither, and that he was bound to take him. Half-witted and mad persons being more holy than others, Ahmet was conveyed to Iskender.

Arriving in Iskender, Hadji Ahmet roamed far and wide, proceeding as far as Cairo, in search of the luxuries he had enjoyed at Constantinople when in the land of Morpheus, which he had been promised to enjoy in the sunshine, if he came to Egypt. Alas! for Hadji Ahmet; the only bread he had to eat was that which was given him by sympathizing humanity. Time sped on, sympathy was growing tired of expending itself on Hadji Ahmet, and his crusts of bread were few and far between.

Wearied of life and suffering, he decided to ask Allah to let him die, and wandering out to the Pyramids he solicited the stones to have pity and fall on him. It happened that a Turk heard this prayer, and said to him:

"Why so miserable, father? Has your soul been so strangled that you prefer its being dashed out of your body, to its remaining the prescribed time in bondage?"

"Yes, my son," said Hadji Ahmet. "Far away in Stamboul, with the help of God, I managed as a junkman to feed my wife and myself; but here am I, in Egypt, a stranger, alone and starving, with possibly my wife already dead of starvation, and all this through a dream."

"Alas! Alas! my father! that you at your age should be tempted to wander so far from home and friends, because of a dream. Why, were I to obey my dreams, I would at this present moment be in Stamboul, digging for a treasure that lies buried under a tree. I can even now, although I have never been there, describe where it is. In my mind's eye I see a wall, a great wall, that must have been built many years ago, and supporting or seeming to support this wall are towers with many corners, towers that are round, towers that are square, and others that have smaller towers within them. In one of these towers, a square one, there live an old man and woman, and close by the tower is a large tree, and every night when I dream of the place, the old man tells me to dig and disclose the treasure. But, father, I am not such a fool as to go to Stamboul and seek to verify this. It is an oft-repeated dream and nothing more. See what you have been reduced to by coming so far."

"Yes," said Hadji Ahmet, "it is a dream and nothing more, but you have interpreted it. Allah be praised, you have encouraged me; I will return to my home."

And Hadji Ahmet and the young stranger parted, the one grateful that it had pleased Allah to give him the power to revive and encourage a drooping spirit, and the other grateful to Allah that when he had despaired of life a stranger should come and give him the interpretation of his dream. He certainly had wandered far and long to learn that the treasure was in his own garden.

Hadji Ahmet in due course, much to the astonishment of both wife and neighbors, again appeared upon the scene not a much changed man. In fact, he was the cinder and iron gatherer of old.

To all questions as to where he was and what he had been doing, he would answer: "A dream sent me away, and a dream brought me back."

And the neighbors would say: "Truly he must be blessed."

One night Hadji Ahmet went to the tree, provided with spade and pick, that he had secured from an obliging neighbor. After digging a short time a heavy case was brought to view, in which he found gold, silver, and precious jewels of great value. Hadji Ahmet replaced the case and earth and returned to bed, much lamenting that it had pleased God to furnish women, more especially his wife, with a long tongue, long hair, and very short wits. Alas! he thought, if I tell my wife, I may be hung as a robber, for it is against the laws of nature for a woman to keep a secret. Yet, becoming more generous when thinking of the years of toil and hardship she had shared with him, he decided to try and see if, by chance, his wife was not an exception to other women. Who knows, she might keep the secret. To test her, at no risk to himself and the treasure, he conceived a plan.

Crawling from his bed, he sallied forth and bought, found, or stole an egg. This egg on the following morning he showed to his wife, and said to her:

"Alas! I fear I am not as other men, for evidently in the night I laid this egg; and, wife mine, if the neighbors hear of this, your husband, the long-suffering Hadji Ahmet, will be bastinadoed, bowstrung, and burned to death. Ah, truly, my soul is strangled."

And without another word Hadji Ahmet, with a sack on his shoulder, went forth to gather the cast-off shoes of horse, ox, or ass, wondering if his wife would prove an exception in this, as she had in many other ways, to other women.

In the evening he returned, heavily laden with his finds, and as he neared home he heard rumors, ominous rumors, that a certain Hadji Ahmet, who had been considered a holy man, had done something that was unknown in the history of man, even in the history of hens — that he had laid a dozen eggs.

Needless to add that Hadji Ahmet did not tell his wife of the treasure, but daily went forth with his sack to gather iron and cinders, and invariably found, when separating his finds of the day, in company with his wife, at first one, and then more gold and silver pieces, and now and then a precious stone.

HOW CHAPKIN HALID BECAME
CHIEF DETECTIVE

n Balata there lived, some years ago, two scapegraces, called Chapkin Halid and Pitch Osman. These two young rascals lived by their wits and at the expense of their neighbors. But they often had to lament the ever-increasing difficulties they encountered in procuring the few piasters they needed daily for bread and the tavern. They had tried several schemes in their own neighborhood, with exceptionally poor results, and were almost disheartened when Chapkin Halid conceived an idea that seemed to offer every chance of success. He explained to his chum Osman that Balata was "played out," at least for a time, and that they must go elsewhere to satisfy their needs. Halid's plan was to go to Stamboul, and feign death in the principal street, while Osman was to collect the funeral expenses of his friend Halid.

Arriving in Stamboul, Halid stretched himself on his back on the pavement and covered his face with an old sack, while Osman sat himself down beside the supposed corpse, and every now and then bewailed the hard fate of the stranger who had met with death on the first day of his arrival. The corpse prompted Osman whenever the coast was clear, and the touching tale told by Osman soon brought contributions for the burial of the stranger. Osman had collected about thirty piasters, and Halid was seriously thinking of a resurrection, but was prevented by the passing of the Grand Vizier, who, upon inquiring why the man lay on the ground in that fashion, was told that he was a stranger who had died in the street. The Grand Vizier thereupon gave instructions to an Imam, who happened to be at hand, to bury the stranger and come for the money to the Sublime Porte.

Halid was reverently carried off to the Mosque, and Osman thought that it was time to leave the corpse to take care of itself. The Imam laid Halid on the marble floor and prepared to wash him prior to interment. He had taken off his turban and long cloak and got ready the water, when he remembered that he had no soap, and immediately went out to purchase some. No sooner had the Imam disappeared than Halid jumped up, and, donning the Imam's turban and long cloak, repaired to the Sublime Porte. Here he asked admittance to the Grand Vizier, but this request was not granted until he told the nature of his business. Halid said he was the Imam who, in compliance with the verbal instructions received from his Highness, had buried a stranger and that he had come for payment. The Grand Vizier sent five gold pieces (twenty piasters each) to the supposed Imam, and Halid made off as fast as possible.

No sooner had Halid departed than the cloakless Imam arrived in breathless haste, and explained that he was the Imam who had received instructions from the Grand Vizier to bury a stranger, but that the supposed corpse had disappeared, and so had his cloak and turban. Witnesses proved this man to be the bona-fide Imam of the quarter, and the Grand Vizier gave orders to his Chief Detective to capture, within three days, on pain of death, and bring to the Sublime Porte, this fearless evil-doer.

The Chief Detective was soon on the track of Halid; but the latter was on the keen lookout. With the aid of the money he had received from the Grand Vizier to defray his burial expenses he successfully evaded the clutches of the Chief Detective, who was greatly put about at being thus frustrated. On the second day he again got scent of Halid and determined to follow him till an opportunity offered for his capture. Halid knew that he was followed and divined the intentions of his pursuer. As he was passing a pharmacy he noticed there several young men, so he entered and explained in Jewish-Spanish (one of his accomplishments) to the Jew druggist, as he handed him one of the gold pieces he had received from the Grand Vizier, that his uncle, who would come in presently, was not right in his mind; but that if the druggist could manage to douche his head and back with cold water, he would be all right for a week or two. No sooner did the Chief Detective enter the shop than, at a word from the apothecary, the young men seized him and, by means of a large squirt, they did their utmost to effectively give him the salutary and cooling douche. The more the detective protested, the more the apothecary consolingly explained that the operation would soon be over and that he would feel much better, and told of the numerous similar cases he had cured in a like manner. The detective saw that it was useless to struggle, so he abandoned himself to the treatment; and in the meantime Halid made off. The Chief Detective was so disheartened that he went to the Grand Vizier and asked him to behead him, as death was preferable to the annoyance he had received and might still receive at the hands of Chapkin Halid. The Grand Vizier was both furious and amused, so he spared the Chief Detective and gave orders that guards be placed at the twenty-four gates of the city, and that Halid be seized at the first opportunity. A reward was further promised to the person who would bring him to the Sublime Porte.

Halid was finally caught one night as he was going out of the Top-Kapou (Cannon Gate), and the guards, rejoicing in their capture, after considerable consultation decided to bind Halid to a large tree close to the Guard house, and thus both avoid the loss of sleep and the anxiety incident to watching over so desperate a character. This was done, and Halid now thought that his case was hopeless. Towards dawn, Halid perceived a man with a lantern walking toward the Armenian Church, and rightly concluded that it was the beadle going to make ready for the early morning service. So he called out in a loud voice:

"Beadle! Brother! Beadle! Brother! come here quickly."

Now it happened that the beadle was a poor hunchback, and no sooner did Halid perceive this than he said:

"Quick! Quick! Beadle, look at my back and see if it has gone!"

"See if what has gone?" asked the beadle, carefully looking behind the tree.

"Why, my hump, of course," answered Halid.

The beadle made a close inspection and declared that he could see no hump.

"A thousand thanks!" fervently exclaimed Halid, "then please undo the rope."

The beadle set about to liberate Halid, and at the same time earnestly begged to be told how he had got rid of the hump, so that he also might free himself of his deformity. Halid agreed to tell him the cure, provided the beadle had not yet broken fast, and also that he was prepared to pay a certain small sum of money for the secret. The beadle satisfied Halid on both of these points, and the latter immediately set about binding the hunchback to the tree, and further told him, on pain of breaking the spell, to repeat sixty-one times the words: 'Esserti! Pesserti! Sersepeti!' if he did this, the hump would of a certainty disappear. Halid left the poor beadle religiously and earnestly repeating the words.

The guards were furious when they found, bound to the tree, a madman, as they thought, repeating incoherent words, instead of Halid. They began to unbind the captive, but the only answer they could get to their host of questions was 'Esserti, Pesserti, Sersepeti.' As the knots were loosened, the louder did the beadle in despair call out the charmed words in the hopes of arresting them. No sooner was the beadle freed than he asked God to bring down calamity on the destroyers of the charm that was to remove his hunch. On hearing the beadle's tale, the guards understood how their prisoner had secured his liberty, and sent word to the Chief Detective. This gentleman told the Grand Vizier of the unheard-of cunning of the escaped prisoner. The Grand Vizier was amused and also very anxious to see this Chapkin Halid, so he sent criers all over the city, giving full pardon to Halid on condition that he would come to the Sublime Porte and confess in person to the Grand Vizier. Halid obeyed the summons, and came to kiss the hem of the Grand Vizier's garment, who was so favorably impressed by him that he then and there appointed him to be his Chief Detective.

HOW COBBLER AHMET BECAME THE CHIEF ASTROLOGER

Every day cobbler Ahmet, year in and year out, measured the breadth of his tiny cabin with his arms as he stitched old shoes. To do this was his Kismet, his decreed fate, and he was content — and why not? his business brought him quite sufficient to provide the necessaries of life for both himself and his wife. And had it not been for a coincidence that occurred, in all probability he would have mended old boots and shoes to the end of his days.

One day cobbler Ahmet's wife went to the Hamam (bath), and while there she was much annoyed at being obliged to give up her compartment, owing to the arrival of the Harem and retinue of the Chief Astrologer to the Sultan. Much hurt, she returned home and vented her pique upon her innocent husband.

"Why are you not the Chief Astrologer to the Sultan?" she said. "I will never call or think of you as my husband until you have been appointed Chief Astrologer to his Majesty."

Ahmet thought that this was another phase in the eccentricity of woman which in all probability would disappear before morning, so he took small notice of what his wife said. But Ahmet was wrong. His wife persisted so much in his giving up his present means of earning a livelihood and becoming an astrologer, that finally, for the sake of peace, he complied with her desire. He sold his tools and collection of sundry old boots and shoes, and, with the proceeds purchased an inkwell and reeds. But this, alas! did not constitute him an astrologer, and he explained to his wife that this mad idea of hers would bring him to an unhappy end. She, however, could not be moved, and insisted on his going to the highway, there to wisely practise the art, and thus ultimately become the Chief Astrologer.

In obedience to his wife's instructions, Ahmet sat down on the highroad, and his oppressed spirit sought comfort in looking at the heavens and sighing deeply. While in this condition a Hanoum in great excitement came and asked him if he communicated with the stars. Poor Ahmet sighed, saying that he was compelled to converse with them.

"Then please tell me where my diamond ring is, and I will both bless and handsomely reward you."

The Hanoum, with this, immediately squatted on the ground, and began to tell Ahmet that she had gone to the bath that morning and that she was positive that she then had the ring, but every corner of the Hamam had been searched, and the ring was not to be found.

"Oh! astrologer, for the love of Allah, exert your eye to see the unseen."

"Hanoum Effendi," replied Ahmet, the instant her excited flow of language had ceased, "I perceive a rent," referring to a tear he had noticed in her shalvars or baggy trousers. Up jumped the Hanoum, exclaiming:

"A thousand holy thanks! You are right! Now I remember! I put the ring in a crevice of the cold water fountain." And in her gratitude she handed Ahmet several gold pieces.

In the evening he returned to his home, and giving the gold to his wife, said: "Take this money, wife; may it satisfy you, and in return all I ask is that you allow me to go back to the trade of my father, and not expose me to the danger and suffering of trudging the road shoeless."

But her purpose was unmoved. Until he became the Chief Astrologer she would neither call him nor think of him as her husband.

In the meantime, owing to the discovery of the ring, the fame of Ahmet the cobbler spread far and wide. The tongue of the Hanoum never ceased to sound his praise.

It happened that the wife of a certain Pasha had appropriated a valuable diamond necklace, and as a last resource, the Pasha determined, seeing that all the astrologers, Hodjas, and diviners had failed to discover the article, to consult Ahmet the cobbler, whose praises were in every mouth.

The Pasha went to Ahmet, and, in fear and trembling, the wife who had appropriated the necklace sent her confidential slave to overhear what the astrologer would say. The Pasha told Ahmet all he knew about the necklace, but this gave no clue, and in despair he asked how many diamonds the necklace contained. On being told that there were twenty-four, Ahmet, to put off the evil hour, said it would take an hour to discover each diamond, consequently would the Pasha come on the morrow at the same hour when, Inshallah, he would perhaps be able to give him some news.

The Pasha departed, and no sooner was he out of earshot, than the troubled Ahmet exclaimed in a loud voice:

"Oh woman! Oh woman! what evil influence impelled you to go the wrong path, and drag others with you! When the twenty-four hours are up, you will perhaps repent! Alas! Too late. Your husband gone from you forever! Without a hope even of being united in paradise."

Ahmet was referring to himself and his wife, for he fully expected to be cast into prison on the following day as an impostor. But the slave who had been listening gave another interpretation to his words, and hurrying off, told her mistress that the astrologer knew all about the theft. The good man had even bewailed the separation that would inevitably take place. The Pasha's wife was distracted, and hurried off to plead her cause in person with the astrologer. On approaching Ahmet, the first words she said, in her excitement, were:

"Oh learned Hodja, you are a great and good man. Have compassion on my weakness and do not expose me to the wrath of my husband! I will do such penance as you may order, and bless you five times daily as long as I live."

"How can I save you?" innocently asked Ahmet. "What is decreed is decreed!"

And then, though silent, looked volumes, for he instinctively knew that words unuttered were arrows still in the quiver.

"If you won't pity me," continued the Hanoum, in despair, "I will go and confess to my Pasha, and perhaps he will forgive me."

To this appeal Ahmet said he must ask the stars for their views on the subject. The Hanoum inquired if the answer would come before the twenty-four hours were up. Ahmet's reply to this was a long and concentrated gaze at the heavens.

"Oh Hodja Effendi, I must go now, or the Pasha will miss me. Shall I give you the necklace to restore to the Pasha without explanation, when he comes to-morrow for the answer?"

Ahmet now realized what all the trouble was about, and in consideration of a fee, he promised not to reveal her theft on the condition that she would at once return home and place the necklace between the mattresses of her Pasha's bed. This the grateful woman agreed to do, and departed invoking blessings on Ahmet, who in return promised to exercise his influence in her behalf for astral intervention.

When the Pasha came to the astrologer at the appointed time, he explained to him, that if he wanted both the necklace and the thief or thieves, it would take a long time, as it was impossible to hurry the stars; but if he would be content with the necklace alone, the horoscope indicated that the stars would oblige him at once. The Pasha said that he would be quite satisfied if he could get his diamonds again, and Ahmet at once told him where to find them. The Pasha returned to his home not a little sceptical, and immediately searched for the necklace where Ahmet had told him it was to be found. His joy and astonishment on discovering the long-lost article knew no bounds, and the fame of Ahmet the cobbler was the theme of every tongue.

Having received handsome payment from both the Pasha and the Hanoum, Ahmet earnestly begged of his wife to desist and not bring down sorrow and calamity upon his head. But his pleadings were in vain. Satan had closed his wife's ear to reason with envy. Resigned to his fate, all he could do was to consult the stars, and after mature thought give their communication, or assert that the stars had, for some reason best known to the applicant, refused to commune on the subject.

It happened that forty cases of gold were stolen from the Imperial Treasury, and every astrologer having failed to get even a clue as to where the money was or how it had disappeared, Ahmet was approached. Poor man, his case now looked hopeless! Even the Chief Astrologer was in disgrace. What might be his punishment he did not know — most probably death. Ahmet had no idea of the numerical importance of forty; but concluding that it must be large he asked for a delay of forty days to discover the forty cases of gold. Ahmet gathered up the implements of his occult art, and before returning to his home, went to a shop and asked for forty beans — neither one more nor one less. When he got home and laid them down before him he appreciated the number of cases of gold that had been stolen, and also the number of days he had to live. He knew it would be useless to explain to his wife the seriousness of the case, so that evening he took from his pocket the forty beans and mournfully said:

"Forty cases of gold, — forty thieves, — forty days; and here is one of them," handing a bean to his wife. "The rest remain in their place until the time comes to give them up."

While Ahmet was saying this to his wife one of the thieves was listening at the window. The thief was sure he had been discovered when he heard Ahmet say, "And here is one of them," and hurried off to tell his companions.

The thieves were greatly distressed, but decided to wait till the next evening and see what would happen then, and another of the number was sent to listen and see if the report would be verified. The listener had not long been stationed at his post when he heard Ahmet say to his wife: "And here is another of them," meaning another of the forty days of his life. But the thief understood the words otherwise, and hurried off to tell his chief that the astrologer knew all about it and knew that he had been there. The thieves consequently decided to send a delegation to Ahmet, confessing their guilt and offering to return the forty cases of gold intact. Ahmet received them, and on hearing their confession, accompanied with their condition to return the gold, boldly told them that he did not require their aid; that it was in his power to take possession of the forty cases of gold whenever he wished, but that he had no special desire to see them all executed, and he would plead their cause if they would go and put the gold in a place he indicated. This was agreed to, and Ahmet continued to give his wife a bean daily — but now with another purpose; he no longer feared the loss of his head, but discounted by degrees the great reward he hoped to receive. At last the final bean was given to his wife, and Ahmet was summoned to the Palace. He went, and explained to his Majesty that the stars refused both to reveal the thieves and the gold, but whichever of the two his Majesty wished would be immediately granted. The Treasury being low, it was decided that, provided the cases were returned with the gold intact, his Majesty would be satisfied. Ahmet conducted them to the place where the gold was buried, and amidst great rejoicing it was taken back to the Palace. The Sultan was so pleased with Ahmet, that he appointed him to the office of Chief Astrologer, and his wife attained her desire.

The Sultan was one day walking in his Palace grounds accompanied by his Chief Astrologer; wishing to test his powers he caught a grasshopper, and holding his closed hand out to the astrologer asked him what it contained. Ahmet, in a pained and reproachful tone, answered the Sultan by a much-quoted proverb: "Alas! Your Majesty! the grasshopper never knows where its third leap will land it," figuratively alluding to himself and the dangerous hazard of guessing what was in the clenched hand of his Majesty. The Sultan was so struck by the reply that Ahmet was never again troubled to demonstrate his powers.

THE WISE SON OF ALI PASHA

A servant of his Majesty Sultan Ahmet, who had been employed for twenty-five years in the Palace, begged leave of the Sultan to allow him to retire to his native home, and at the same time solicited a pension to enable him to live. The Sultan asked him if he had not saved any money. The man replied that owing to his having to support a large family, he had been unable to do so. The Sultan was very angry that any of his servants, especially in the immediate employ of his household, should, after so many years' service, say that he was penniless. Disbelieving the statement, and in order to make an example, the Sultan gave orders that Hassan should quit the Palace in the identical state he had entered it twenty-five years before. Hassan was accordingly disrobed of all his splendor, and his various effects, the accumulation of a quarter of a century, were confiscated, and distributed amongst the legion of Palace servants. Poor Hassan, without a piaster in his pocket, and dressed in the rude costume of his native province, began his weary journey homeward on foot.

In time he reached the suburbs of a town in Asia Minor, and seeing some boys playing, he approached them, sat on the ground, and watched their pastime. The boys were playing at state affairs: one was a Sultan, another his Vizier, who had his cabinet of Ministers, while close by were a number of boys bound hand and foot, representing political and other prisoners, awaiting judgment for their imaginary misdeeds. The Sultan, who was sitting with worthy dignity on a throne made of branches and stones, decorated with many-colored centrepieces, beckoned to Hassan to draw near, and asked him where he had come from. Hassan replied that he had come from Stamboul, from the Palace of the Sultan.

"That's a lie," said the mock Sultan, "no one ever came from Stamboul dressed in that fashion, much less from the Palace; you are from the far interior, and if you do not confess that what I say is true, you will be tried by my Ministers, and punished accordingly."

Hassan, partly to participate in their boyish amusement, and partly to unburden his aching heart, related his sad fate to his youthful audience. When he had finished, the boy Sultan, Ali by name, asked him if he had received his twenty-five years. Hassan, not fully grasping what the boy said, replied:

"Nothing! Nothing!"

"That is unjust," continued Ali, "and you shall go back to the Sultan and ask that your twenty-five years be returned to you so that you may plough and till your ground, and thus make provision for the period of want, old age."

Hassan was struck by the sound advice the boy had given him, thanked him and said he would follow it to the letter. The boys then in thoughtless mirth separated, to return to their homes, never dreaming that the seeds of destiny of one of their number had been sown in play. Hassan, retracing his steps, reappeared in time at the gates of the Palace and begged admittance, stating that he had forgotten to communicate something of importance to his Majesty. His request being granted, he humbly solicited, that, inasmuch as his Majesty had been dissatisfied with his long service, the twenty-five years he had devoted to him should be returned, so that he might labor and put by something to provide for the inevitable day when he could no longer work. The Sultan answered:

"That is well said and just. As it is not in my power to give you the twenty-five years, the best equivalent I can grant you is the means of sustenance for a period of that duration should you live so long. But tell me, who advised you to make this request?"

Hassan then related his adventure with the boys while on his journey home, and his Majesty was so pleased with the judgment and advice of the lad that he sent for him and had him educated. The boy studied medicine, and distinguishing himself in the profession ultimately rose to be Hekim Ali Pasha.

He had one son who was known as Doctor Ali Pasha's son. He studied calligraphy, and became so proficient in this art, now almost lost, that his imitations of the Imperial Iradés (decrees) were perfect fac-similes of the originals. One day he took it into his head to write an Iradé appointing himself Grand Vizier, in place of the reigning one, a protégé of the Imperial Palace, which Iradé he took to the Sublime Porte and there and then installed himself. By chance the Sultan happened to drive through Stamboul that day, in disguise, and noticing considerable excitement and cries of "Padishahim chok yasha" (long live my Sultan) amongst the people, made inquiries as to the cause of this unusual occurrence. His Majesty's informers brought him the word that the people rejoiced in the fall of the old Grand Vizier, and the appointment of the new one, Doctor

Ali Pasha's son. The Sultan returned to the Palace and immediately sent one of his eunuchs to the Sublime Porte to see the Grand Vizier and find out the meaning of these strange proceedings.

The eunuch was announced, and the Grand Vizier ordered him to be brought into his presence. Directly he appeared in the doorway, he was greeted with: "What do you want, you black dog?"

Then turning to the numerous attendants about, he said: "Take this nigger to the slave market, and see what price he will bring."

The eunuch was taken to the slave market, and the highest price bid for him was fifty piasters. On hearing this, the Grand Vizier turned to the eunuch and said: "Go and tell your master what you are worth, and tell him that I think it too much by far."

The eunuch was glad to get off, and communicated to his Majesty the story of his strange treatment. The Sultan then ordered his Chief Eunuch, a not unimportant personage in the Ottoman Empire, to call on the Grand Vizier for an explanation. At the Sublime Porte, however, no respect was paid to this high dignitary. Ali Pasha received him in precisely the same manner as he had received his subordinate. The chief was taken to the slave market, and the highest sum bid for him was five hundred piasters. The self-appointed Grand Vizier ordered him to go and tell his master the amount some foolish people were willing to pay for him.

When the Sultan heard of these strange proceedings he sent an autograph letter to Ali Pasha, commanding him to come to the Palace. The Grand Vizier immediately set out for the Palace and was received in audience, when he explained to his Majesty that the affairs of State could not be managed by men not worth more than from fifty to five hundred piasters, and that if radical changes were not made, certain ruin would be the outcome. The Sultan appreciated this earnest communication, and ratified the appointment, as Grand Vizier, of Ali Pasha, the son of the boy who had played at state affairs in a village of Asia Minor.

THE MERCIFUL KHAN

here lived once near Ispahan a tailor, a hard-working man, who was very poor. So poor was he that his workshop and house together consisted of a wooden cottage of but one room.

But poverty is no protection against thieves, and so it happened that one night a thief entered the hut of the tailor. The tailor had driven nails in various places in the walls on which to hang the garments that were brought to him to mend. It chanced that in groping about for plunder, the thief struck against one of these nails and put out his eye.

The next morning the thief appeared before the Khan (Judge) and demanded justice. The Khan accordingly sent for the tailor, stated the complaint of the thief, and said that in accordance with the law, 'an eye for an eye,' it would be necessary to put out one of the tailor's eyes. As usual, however, the tailor was allowed to plead in his own defence, whereupon he thus addressed the court:

"Oh great and mighty Khan, it is true that the law says *an* eye for an eye, but it does not say *my* eye. Now I am a poor man, and a tailor. If the Khan puts out one of my eyes, I will not be able to carry on my trade, and so I shall starve. Now it happens that there lives near me a gunsmith. He uses but one eye with which he squints along the barrel of his guns. Take his other eye, oh Khan, and let the law be satisfied."

The Khan was favorably impressed with this idea, and accordingly sent for the gunsmith. He recited to the gunsmith the complaint of the thief and the statement of the tailor, whereupon the gun-smith said:

"Oh great and mighty Khan, this tailor knows not whereof he talks. I need both of my eyes; for while it is true that I squint one eye along one side of the barrel of the gun, to see if it is straight, I must use the other eye for the other side. If, therefore, you put out one of my eyes you will take away from me the means of livelihood. It happens, however, that there lives not far from me a flute-player. Now I have noticed that whenever he plays the flute he closes both of his eyes. Take out one of his eyes, oh Khan, and let the law be satisfied."

Accordingly, the Khan sent for the flute-player, and after reciting to him the complaint of the thief, and the words of the gunsmith, he ordered him to play upon his flute. This the flute-player did, and though he endeavored to control himself, he did not succeed, but, as the result of long habit, closed both of his eyes. When the Khan saw this, he ordered that one of the flute-player's eyes be put out, which being done, the Khan spoke as follows:

"Oh flute-player, I saw that when playing upon your flute you closed both of your eyes. It was thus clear to me that neither was necessary for your livelihood, and I had intended to have them both put out, but I have decided to put out only one in order that you may tell among men how merciful are the Khans."

KING KARA-KUSH OF BITHYNIA

King of Bithynia, named Kara-kush, who was blind of an eye, was considered in his day a reasonable, just, and feeling man. He administered justice upon the basis of the law, 'An eye for an eye, a tooth for a tooth,' and enlarged or modified it as circumstances demanded.

It happened that a weaver by accident put out the eye of a man. He was brought before the King or Cadi, for in those days the Kings acted as Cadis, who promptly condemned him, in accordance with the law, to the loss of an eye. The weaver pleaded touchingly, saying:

"Oh Cadi! I have a wife and a large family, and I support them by throwing the shuttle from the right to the left, and again from the left to the right; first using the one eye and then the other. If you remove one of my eyes, I will not be able to weave, and my wife and children will suffer the pangs of hunger. Why not, in the place of my eye, remove that of the hunter who uses but one eye in exercising his profession, and to whom two eyes are superfluous?"

The Cadi was impressed, acknowledged the justice of the weaver's remarks, and the hunter was immediately sent for. The hunter being brought, the Cadi was greatly rejoiced to notice that the hunter's eyes were exactly the same color as his own. He asked the hunter how he earned his living, and receiving his answer that he was a hunter, the Cadi asked him how he shot. The hunter in reply demonstrated the manner by putting up his arms, his head to a side, and closing one eye. The Cadi said the weaver was right, and immediately sent for the surgeon to have the eye removed. Further, the Cadi bethought him that he might profit by this and have the hunter's eye placed in his own socket. The surgeon set to work and prepared the cavity to receive the hunter's eye. This done with a practised hand, the surgeon removed the hunter's eye and was about to place it in the prepared socket, when it accidentally slipped from his fingers to the ground, and was snatched up by a cat. The surgeon was terrified and madly ran after the cat; but alas! the cat had eaten the eye. What was he to do? On the inspiration of the moment he snatched out the eye of the cat, and placing it in the Cadi's head, bound it up.

Some time after the surgeon asked the Cadi how he saw.

"Oh," replied the Cadi, "with my old eye I see as usual, but strange to say, the new eye you placed in my head is continually searching and watching for rat holes."

THE PRAYER RUG AND THE DISHONEST STEWARD

poor Hamal (porter) brought to the Pasha of Stamboul his savings, consisting of a small canvas bag of medjidies (Turkish silver dollars), to be kept for him, while he was absent on a visit to his home. The Pasha, being a kind-hearted man, consented, and after sealing the bag, called his steward, instructing him to keep it till the owner called for it. The steward gave the man a receipt, to the effect that he had received a sealed bag containing money.

When the poor man returned, he went to the Pasha and received his bag of money. On reaching his room he opened the bag, and to his horror found that it contained, instead of the medjidies he had put in it, copper piasters, which are about the same size as medjidies. The poor Hamal was miserable, his hard-earned savings gone.

He at last gathered courage to go and put his case before the Pasha. He took the bag of piasters, and with trembling voice and faltering heart he assured the Pasha that though he had received his bag apparently intact, on opening it he found that it contained copper piasters and not the medjidies he had put in it. The Pasha took the bag, examined it closely, and after some time noticed a part that had apparently been darned by a master-hand. The Pasha told the Hamal to go away and come back in a week; in the meantime he would see what he could do for him. The grateful man departed, uttering prayers for the life and prosperity of his Excellency.

The next morning after the Pasha had said his prayers kneeling on a most magnificent and expensive rug, he took a knife and cut a long rent in it. He then left his Konak without saying a word to any one. In the evening when he returned he found that the rent had been so well repaired that it was with difficulty that he discovered where it had been. Calling his steward, he demanded who had repaired his prayer rug. The steward told the Pasha that he thought the rug had been cut by accident by some of the servants, so he had sent to the Bazaar for the darner, Mustapha, and had it mended, the steward, by way of apology, adding that it was very well done.

"Send for Mustapha immediately," said the Pasha, "and when he comes bring him to my room."

When Mustapha arrived, the Pasha asked him if he had repaired the rug. Mustapha at once replied that he had mended it that very morning.

"It is indeed well done," said the Pasha; "much better than the darn you made in that canvas bag."

Mustapha agreed, saying that it was very difficult to mend the bag as it was full of copper piasters. On hearing this, the Pasha gave him a backsheesh (present) and told him to retire. The Pasha then called his steward, and not only compelled him to pay the Hamal his money, but discharged him from his service, in which he had been engaged for many years.

THE GOOSE, THE EYE, THE DAUGH-
TER, AND THE ARM

A Turk decided to have a feast, so he killed and stuffed a goose and took it to the baker to be roasted. The Cadi of the village happened to pass by the oven as the baker was basting the goose, and was attracted by the pleasant and appetizing odor. Approaching the baker, the Cadi said it was a fine goose; that the smell of it made him quite hungry, and suggested that he had better send it to his house. The baker expostulated, saying: "I cannot; it does not belong to me."

The Cadi assured him that was no difficulty. "You tell Ahmet, the owner of the goose, that it flew away."

"Impossible!" said the baker. "How can a roasted goose fly away? Ahmet will only laugh at me, your Worship, and I will be cast into prison."

"Am I not a Judge?" said the Cadi, "fear nothing."

At this the baker consented to send the goose to the Cadi's house. When Ahmet came for his goose the baker said: "Friend, thy goose has flown."

"Flown?" said Ahmet, "what lies! Am I thy grandfather's grandchild that thou shouldst laugh in my beard?"

Seizing one of the baker's large shovels, he lifted it to strike him, but, as fate would have it, the handle put out the eye of the baker's boy, and Ahmet, frightened at what he had done, ran off, closely followed by the baker and his boy, the latter crying:

"My eye!"

In his hurry Ahmet knocked over a child, killing it, and the father of the child joined in the chase, calling out: "My daughter!"

Ahmet, well-nigh distracted, rushed into a mosque and up a minaret. To escape his pursuers he leaped from the parapet, and fell upon a vender who was passing by, breaking his arm. The vender also began pursuing him, calling out: "My arm!"

Ahmet was finally caught and brought before the Cadi, who no doubt was feeling contented with the world, having just enjoyed the delicious goose.

The Cadi heard each of the cases brought against Ahmet, who in turn told his case truthfully as it had happened.

"A complicated matter," said the Cadi. "All these misfortunes come from the flight of the goose, and I must refer to the book of the law to give just judgment."

Taking down a ponderous manuscript volume, the Cadi turned to Ahmet and asked him what number egg the goose had been hatched from. Ahmet said he did not know.

"Then," replied the Cadi, "the book writes that such a phenomenon was possible. If this goose was hatched from the seventh egg, and the hatcher also from the seventh egg, the book writes that it is possible for a roasted goose, under those conditions, to fly away."

"With reference to your eye," continued the Cadi, addressing the baker's lad, "the book provides punishment for the removal of two eyes, but not of one, so if you will consent to your other eye being taken out, I will condemn Ahmet to have both of his removed."

The baker's lad, not appreciating the force of this argument, withdrew his claim.

Then turning to the father of the dead child, the Cadi explained that the only provision for a case like this in the book of the law, was that he take Ahmet's child in its place, or if Ahmet had not a child, to wait till he got one. The bereaved parent not taking any interest in Ahmet's present or prospective children, also withdrew his case.

These cases settled, there remained but the vender's, who was wroth at having his arm broken. The Cadi expatiated on the justice of the law and its far-seeing provisions, that the vender at least could claim ample compensation for having his arm broken. The book of the law provided that he should go to the very same minaret, and that Ahmet must station himself at the very same place where he had stood when his arm was broken; and that he might jump down and break Ahmet's arm.

"But be it understood," concluded the Cadi, "if you break his leg instead of his arm, Ahmet will have the right to delegate some one to jump down on you to break your leg."

The vender not seeing the force of the Cadi's proposal, also withdrew his claim.

Thus ended the cases of the goose, the eye, the daughter, and the arm.

THE FORTY WISE MEN

In a day amongst the many days, when the Turk was more earnest than now, before the Europeans came and gave new ideas to our children, there lived and labored for the welfare of our people an organized body of men. At whose suggestion this society was formed I know not. All that we know of them to-day, through our fathers, is that their forefathers chose from among them the most wise, sincere, and experienced forty brethren. These forty were named the Forty Wise Men. When one of the forty was called away from his labors here, perhaps to continue them in higher spheres, or to receive his reward, who knows? the remaining thirty-nine consulted and chose from the community him whom they thought capable, and worthy of guiding and of being guided, to add to their number. They lived and held their meetings in a mosque of which little remains now, the destructive hand of time having left it but a battered dome, with cheerless walls and great square holes, where once were iron bars and stained glass. It has gone — so have the wise men. But its foundations are solid, and they may in time come to support an edifice dedicated to noble work, and, Inshallah, the seed of the Forty Wise Men will also bear fruit in the days that are not yet.

You will say, what good did this body of men do? These men who always numbered forty were, as I have told you, originally chosen by the people, and when one of the forty departed from his labors here, the remaining thirty-nine consulted together and from the most worthy of the community they chose another member.

What was the good of this body of men? Great, great, my friends. Not only did they administer justice to the oppressed, and give to the needy substantial aid; but their very existence had the most beneficial effect on the community. Why? you ask. Because each vied with the other to be worthy of being nominated for the vacancy when it occurred. No station in life was too low to be admitted, no station was too high for one of the faithful to become one of the 'Forty.' Here all were equal. As Allah himself doth consider mankind by deeds, so also mankind was considered by the Forty Wise Men, who presided over the welfare and smoothed the destiny of the children of Allah. With their years, their wisdom grew, and they were blessed by Allah.

*****

In the town of Scutari, over the way, there lived and labored a Dervish. His counsel to the rash was ever ready, his sole object, apparently, in life was to become one of the Forty Wise Men, who presided over the people and protected them from all ills.

The years went on, and still without a reward he patiently labored, no doubt contenting himself with the idea that the day would come when the merit of his actions would be recognized by Allah. That was a mistake, my friends; true faith expecteth nothing. However, the day did come, and the Dervish's great desire had every appearance of being realized. One of the Forty Wise Men having accomplished his mission on earth, departed this life. The remaining thirty-nine, who still had duties to fulfil, consulted as to whom they should call to aid them in their work. A eulogy was pronounced in favor of the Dervish. They not unjustly considered how he had labored among the poor in Scutari; ever ready to help the needy, ever ready to counsel the rash, ever ready to comfort and encourage the despairing. It was decided that he should be nominated. A deputation consisting of three, two to listen, one to speak, was named, and with the blessing of their brethren, for success, they entered a caique and were rowed to Scutari. Arriving at the Dervish's gate, the spokesman thus addressed the would-be member of the Forty Wise Men:

"Brother in the flesh, thy actions have been noted, and we come to put a proposition to thee, which, after consideration, thou wilt either accept or reject as thou thinkest best for all interested therein. We would ask thee to become one of us. We are sent hither by, and are the representatives of, the sages who preside over the people. Brother, we number in all one hundred and thirty-eight in spirit; — ninety-nine, having accomplished their task in the flesh, have departed; thirty-nine, still in the flesh, endeavor their duty to fulfil. And it is the desire of the one hundred and thirty-eight souls to add to us thyself, in order to complete our number of laborers in the flesh. Brother, thy duties, which will be everlasting, thou wilt learn when with us. Do thou consider, and we will return at the setting of the sun of the third day, to receive thy answer."

And they turned to depart. But the Dervish stopped them, saying: "Brothers, I have no need to consider the subject for three days, seeing that my inmost desire for thirty years, and my sole object in life has been to become worthy of being one of you. In spirit I have long been your brother, in the flesh it is easy to comply, seeing that it has been the spirit's desire."

Then answered the spokesman: "Brother, thou

hast spoken well. Allah, thou art with us in our choice; we praise Thee. Brother, one word! Our ways are different to all men's ways; thou hast but to have faith, and all is well."

"Brethren, faith! I have had faith; my faith is now even strengthened. I do your bidding."

"Brother, first of all thy worldly goods must be disposed of and rendered into gold. Every earthly possession thou hast must be represented by a piece of gold. Therefore see to that; we have other duties to fulfil, but will return ere the sun sets in the west."

The Dervish set about selling all his goods; and when the coloring of the sky in the west harbingered the closing of the day, he had disposed of everything and stood waiting with naught but a sack of gold.

The three wise men returned, and, on seeing the Dervish, said: "Brother, thou hast done well; we will hence."

A caique was in waiting, and the four entered. Silently the caique glided over the smooth surface of the Bosphorus; and silently the occupants sat. When beyond Maidens' Tower, the spokesman, turning to the Dervish, said: "Brother, with thy inmost blessing give me that sack, representing everything thou dost possess in this world."

The Dervish handed the sack as he was bidden, and the wise man solemnly rose, and holding it on high, said: "With the blessing of our brother Mustapha," and dropped it where the current is strongest. Then, sitting down, resumed his silence. The deed was done, and nothing outward told the story; the Caiquedji dipped his oars, and the waves rippled as soft as before. Nothing but the distant, soothing cry of the Muezzin, calling the faithful to prayer, now waxing, now waning, now completely dying away as they moved around the minarets, broke the stillness.

Ere long the boat was brought to the shore, the four men wended their way up the steep hill, and the horizon, wrapped in the mantle of night, hid them from the boatman's sight. A few minutes' walk brought them to the mosque of the Forty Wise Men; the spokesman turned to the Dervish, and said: "Brother, faithfully follow," and then passed through the doorway. They entered a large, vaulted chamber, the ceiling of which was artistically inlaid with mosaïques, and the floor covered with tiles of the ceramic art of bygone ages. From the centre hung a large chandelier holding a number of little oil cups, each shedding its tiny light, as if to show that union was strength. Round this chandelier were seven brass filagreed, hemispherical-shaped lanterns, holding several oil burners. These many tiny burners gave a soothing, contented, though undefined light, which, together with the silence, added to the impressiveness of the place. Round this hall were forty boxes of the same shape and size.

Our friend stood in the centre of the hall and under the influence of the scene, he was afraid to breathe; he did not know whether to be happy or sad, for having come so far.

As he stood thus thinking, dreaming, one of the curtains was raised, and there came forth a very old man, his venerable white beard all but touching his girdle.

Solemnly and slowly he walked over to the opposite side, and following in his train came thirty-eight more, the last apparently being the youngest.

Chill after chill went coursing down the spinal cord of the astonished would-be brother, whilst these men moved about in the unbroken silence, as if talking to invisible beings; now embracing, now clasping hands, now bidding farewell.

The Dervish closed his eyes, opened them, Were these things so? Yes, it was no dream, no hallucination. Yet why heard he no sound?

Each of the brethren now took his place beside a box, but there was one vacancy; no one stood at the side of the box to the left of the youngest brother. Making a profound salaam, which all answered, the old man silently turned, raised the curtain, and passed into the darkness, each in his order following. As one in a trance, the Dervish watched one after another disappear. The last now raised the curtain, but before vanishing, turned (it was the spokesman), and whispered: "Brother, faith, follow!" and stepped into the darkness.

These words acted upon the Dervish like a spell; he followed.

Up, up, the winding stairway of a minaret they go. At last they arrive, and to the horror of the Dervish, what does he see? One, two, three, disappear over the parapet, and his friend the spokesman, with: "Brother, faith, follow!" also vanished into the inky darkness.

Again at the eleventh hour did the cheering words of the brother spokesman act upon the Dervish like magic, he raised his foot to the parapet, and, in faltering decision, jumped up two or three times. But man's guardian does not lead him over the rugged paths of life; he gives the impulse and you must go. So it was with the Dervish. He jumped once, twice, thrice, but each time fell backward instead of forward. My friends, he hesitated again; at the eleventh hour he was encouraged, but undecided — he was not equal to the test. So, with a great weight on his heart, he descended the winding stairs of the minaret. He had reached his zenith only in desire, and was now on his decline.

Lamenting, like a weak mortal that he was, for not having followed, he again entered the hall he had just left, with the intention, no doubt, of departing.

But the charm of the place was on him again, and as he stood the curtain moved, and the old man advanced; and as before, the silence was unbroken. Again did each take his place beside a box, again did the old man salaam, with the simultaneous response of the others. Again did they gesture as if talking to invisible beings of some calamity which had befallen them which they all regretted.

The old man went and opened the box that stood alone. From this he took, what? the identical bag of gold that had been dropped into the Bosphorus some hours ago. The spokesman came forward and took it from the hand of the old man. The Dervish now no longer believed that *he* was *he* himself, and that these things were taking place. He understood not, he knew not.

Coming forward, the spokesman thus addressed the spell-bound Dervish, his voice giving a strange echo, as if his words were emphasized by a hundred invisible mouths:

"Friend and brother in the flesh, but weak of the spirit, thou hast proved thyself unworthy to impart that which thou hast not thyself, — Faith!

Thine actions hitherto, of seeming conviction, have not been for the eye of the Almighty, the All-seeing, the All-powerful alone, but for the approbation of mankind. To get this approbation thou hast soared out of thine element; the atmosphere is too rarified, thou canst not live, thou must return!

"Get thee back into the world, back to thy brothers; thou canst not be one of us. One hundred and thirty-nine in the spirit have regretfully judged thee as lacking in faith, and not having a sheltered apartment within thyself, thou canst not shelter others. No man can bequeath that which he hath not. Go thy way, and in secret build thee a wall, brick by brick, action by action; let none see thy place but the eye that seeth all, lest a side, when all but completed, fall, and thou art again exposed to the four winds. Take thy money, thine all, and when hesitation interrupts, offer a prayer in thy heart, and then faithfully follow! Farewell!"

And the Dervish was led out into the street, a lone and solitary man; he had his all in his hand — a bag of gold.

HOW THE PRIEST KNEW THAT IT
WOULD SNOW

A Turk travelling in Asia Minor came to a Christian village. He journeyed on horseback, was accompanied by a black slave, and seeming a man of consequence, the priest of the village offered him hospitality for the night. The first thing to be done was to conduct the traveller to the stable, that he might see his horse attended to and comfortably stalled for the night. In the stable was a magnificent Arab horse, belonging to the priest, and the Turk gazed upon it with covetous eyes, but nevertheless, in order that no ill should befall the beautiful creature and to counteract the influence of the evil eye with certainty, he spat at the animal. After they had dined, the priest took his guest for a walk in the garden, and in the course of a very pleasant conversation he informed the Turk that on the morrow there would be snow on the ground.

"Never! Impossible!" said the Turk.

"Well, to-morrow you will see that I am right," said the priest.

"I am willing to stake my horse against yours, that you are wrong," answered the Turk, who was delighted at this opportunity which gave him a chance of securing the horse, without committing the breach in Oriental etiquette of asking his host if he would sell it. After some persuasion the priest accepted his wager, and they separated for the night.

Later on that night, the Turk said to his slave: "Go, Sali, go and see what the weather says, for truly my life is in want of our good host's horse."

Sali went out to make an observation, and on returning said to his master: "Master, the heavens are like unto your face, — without a frown and many kindly sparkling eyes, and the earth is like unto that of your black slave."

"'Tis well, Sali, 'tis well. What a beautiful animal that is!"

Later on, before retiring to rest, he sent his slave on another inspection, and was gratified to receive the same answer. Early in the morning he awoke, and calling his slave, who had slept at his door, he sent him forth again to see if any change had taken place.

"Oh master!" reported Sali, in trembling tones, "Nature has reversed herself, for the heavens are now like the scowling face of your slave, and the earth is like yours, white, entirely white."

"Chok shai! wonderful thing. Then I have lost not only that beautiful animal but my own horse as well. Oh pity! Oh pity!"

He gave up his horse, but before parting he begged the priest to tell him how he knew it would snow.

"My pig told me as we were walking in the garden yesterday. I saw it put its nose in the heap of manure you see in that corner, and I knew that to be a sure sign that it would snow on the morrow," replied the priest.

Deeply mystified, the Turk and his slave proceeded on foot. Reaching a Turkish village before nightfall, he sought and obtained shelter for the night from the Imam, the Mohammedan priest of the village. While partaking of the evening meal he asked the Imam when the feast of the Bairam would be.

"Truly, I do not know! When the cannons fire, I will know it is Bairam," said his host.

"What!" said the traveller, becoming angry, "you an Imam, — a learned Hodja, — and don't know when it will be Bairam, and the pig of the Greek priest knew when it would snow? Shame! Shame!"

And becoming much angered, he declined the hospitality of the Imam and went elsewhere.

WHO WAS THE THIRTEENTH SON

In the town of Adrianople there lived an Armenian Patriarch, Munadi Hagop by name, respected and loved alike by Mussulman and Christian. He was a man of wide reading and profound judgment. The Ottoman Governor of the same place, Usref Pasha, happened also to be a man of considerable acquirements and education. The Armenian and the Turk associated much together. In fact, they were always either walking out together or visiting, one at the residence of the other. This went on for some time, and the twelve wise men who were judges in the city thought that their Governor was doing wrong in associating so much with a dog of a Christian; so they resolved to call him to account.

This resolution taken, the entire twelve proceeded to the house of the Governor and told him that he was setting a bad example to his subjects. They feared, too, that the salvation of his own soul and of his posterity was in danger, should this Armenian in any way influence his mind.

"My friends," answered the Governor, "this man is very learned, and the only reason why we so often come together is because a great sympathy exists between us, and much mutual pleasure is derived from this friendship. I ask his advice, and he gives me a clear explanation. He is my friend, and I would gladly see him your friend."

"Oh," said the spokesman of the judges, "it is his wise answers that act as magic upon you? We will give him a question to answer, and if he solves this to our satisfaction, he will then in reality be a great man."

"I am sure you will not be disappointed!" said the Pasha. "He has never failed me, and I have sometimes put questions to him which appeared unanswerable. He will surely call to-morrow. Shall I send him to you or bring him myself?"

"We wish to see him alone," said the judges.

"I shall not fail to send him to you to-morrow, after which I am sure you will often seek his company."

On the following day the Pasha told the Patriarch how matters stood, and begged him to call on the gentlemen who took so lively an interest in their friendly association.

The Patriarch, never dreaming of what would happen, called on the twelve wise men and introduced himself. They were holding the Divan, and the entrance of the Patriarch gave considerable pleasure to them. On the table lay a turban and a drawn sword.

The customary salutations having been duly exchanged, the Patriarch seated himself, and at once told them that his friend the Governor had asked him to call, and he took much pleasure in making their acquaintance, adding that he would be happy to do anything in his power that they might wish.

The spokesman of the Divan rose and said: "Effendi, our friend the Governor has told us of your great learning, and we have decided to put a question to you. The reason of our taking this liberty is because the Governor told us that he had never put a question to you which had remained unanswered."

And as he spoke he moved toward the table.

"Effendi, our question will consist of only a few words." And laying his right hand on the turban and his left hand on the sword, he said: "Is this the right, or is this the right?"

The Patriarch paused aghast at the terrible feature of the interrogation. He saw destruction staring him in the face. Nevertheless he said to them with great composure: "Gentlemen, you have put an exceedingly difficult question to me, the most difficult that could be put to man. However, it is a question put, and now, according to your laws, cannot be recalled."

"No," answered the twelve wise men, rubbing their hands, "it cannot be recalled."

"I will but say that it grieves me much to have to reply to this," the Patriarch continued, "and I cannot do so without continued prayers for guidance. Therefore I beg to request a week's time before giving my answer."

To this no objection was made, and the Patriarch prepared to go. Respectfully bowing to all present, as if nothing out of the common had happened, he slowly moved toward the door apparently in deep thought.

Just as he reached the door he turned back and addressing the judges, said:

"Gentlemen, one of the reasons I had great pleasure in meeting you to-day was because I wished to have your advice on a difficult legal problem which has been presented to me by some members of my community. Knowing your great wisdom, I thought you might assist me, and as you are now sitting in lawful council I shall, if agreeable to you, put the case before you and be greatly pleased to learn your opinion."

The judges, whose curiosity was aroused, and who were flattered that a man of such reputation for wisdom should submit a matter to them for their opinion, signified to him to proceed.

"Gentlemen and wise men," began the Patriarch, "there was once a father, and this father had thirteen sons, who were esteemed by all who knew them. As time with sure hand marked its progress on the issue of this good man, and the children grew into youth, they one by one went into the world, spreading to the four known quarters of the globe, and carrying with them the good influence given by their father. Through them the name of the father spread, causing a great moral and mental revolution throughout the world. The father in his native home, however, saw that his days were few, that he had well-nigh turned the leaves of the book of life, and yearned to see his sons once more. He accordingly sent messengers all over the world, saying: 'Come, my sons, and receive your father's blessing; he is about to depart this life, come and get each one your portion of the worldly possessions I have, together with my blessing, and again go forth, doing each your duty to God and man.'

"One by one the sons of the aged father came, and once more were united in the ancient home of their childhood, with the exception of one son. The remaining days of the old man were spent with his twelve sons, and the brothers found that all of them had retained the teachings of infancy, and the pleasure was great. The reuniting of the family, though of comparatively short duration, was happier by far than the years of childhood and youth which they had spent together. Still the thirteenth son was not found. The messengers returned one after the other, bearing no tidings of him. The old father saw that he could wait no longer, that he must dispose of his worldly possessions, give his blessing to his twelve sons and rejoin his Father. So he called them to his side and thus spoke to them:

"'My sons, as you have done may it be done unto you. You have cheered my last steps to the grave, and I bless you.'

"And the father's blessing was bestowed on each.

"'Of all I possess I give to each of you an equal share with my blessing. You are my offspring and the representatives of your father on earth. It is my will that you should continue as you have begun. You are my twelve sons, and I have no other. Your brother who was, is no longer. We have waited long, that he should take his portion and my blessing; but he has tarried elsewhere, and now the hand of my Father is on me, and as you have come to me, so I must go to show Him my work.'

"So the father ordained that the twelve should be his heirs, and declared that any one coming after claiming to be his son, was an impostor. He also confirmed in the existing and competent courts that these alone were his representatives on earth. This was duly registered in conformity with the law, and the old father passed away to rejoin his forefathers.

"The twelve sons again went forth into the world and carried with them the blessings and teachings of their father, and these teachings and ideas developed and grew, and the memory of their father was cherished and blessed.

"Many years after, a person turned up claiming to be the missing son, and sought to obtain the part due to him. Not only did he wish his share, but he claimed the whole worldly possessions of his father, that he was the son blessed by his father, and exhorted all to follow his teachings. By those who knew the circumstances, he was not believed; but many were ignorant of the father, and also ignorant of the registering in the courts of law, and were inclined to believe in the impostor.

"Now, gentlemen, this is the case that has troubled me much. As you are sitting in lawful council, it would give me much pleasure if you could cast light on the case. Your statement will help me, and I will be ever grateful to you. Had this son, the late returned person, any right to all the worldly possessions of the father, or, in fact, even any right to an equal share?"

Thus having spoken he turned to the Hodjas with an inquiring look. They one and all, unanimously, and in a breath said, that all the legal formalities having been carried out, the will of the father was law, and the law he passed should be respected, therefore the thirteenth son was an impostor. On returning he should have gone to his brothers, and no doubt he would have been received as a brother, but he acted otherwise. He should receive nothing.

"I am glad to see that you look at it in that light, and I will now say that that has always been my opinion, but your statement now adds strength to the conviction, and had there been any doubt on my part, your unanimous declaration would have dispelled it. I would further esteem it a great kindness and a favor if, as a reference and as a proof of my authority, or rather as a corroboration of many proofs, you would, as you are sitting in lawful Divan, give your signatures to the effect that the decision of the learned council was unanimous, and to this said effect, that the thirteenth son was an impostor, and had no right to any of the possessions he claimed."

Flattered that their opinion had such weight, the judges also consented to do this, and the Patriarch set about drawing up the case. This he read to them, and each put his hand and seal to the document.

The Patriarch thanked them and departed.

A week had passed, and the judges had entirely forgotten the case that had been put to them, but they had not forgotten the Patriarch, and eagerly awaited his answer to their question which left no alternative, and which would cause his head to be separated from his body by a blow of the executioner. But the Patriarch did not make his appearance, and as the prescribed time had passed, the judges went to the Governor to see what steps should be taken.

The Governor was deeply grieved when the judges told him of the terrible question they had put to the Patriarch, yet remembering leaving that morning the Patriarch who had been with him, and who seemed in no wise anxious, he said that he was convinced that either a satisfactory answer had been given or would be forthcoming. He questioned the Hodjas as to what had taken place, and they answered that nothing had been said beyond the question that had been put to him and his request for a week's time in which to answer.

"Did he say nothing at all," asked the Pasha, "before he left?"

"Nothing," said the spokesman of the judges, "except that he put to us a case which he had been called on to decide and asked our opinion."

"What was this case?" asked the Pasha. And the judges recited it to him, told what opinion they had given, and stated that they had, at the Patriarch's request and for his use, placed their seal to this opinion.

"Go home, you heads of asses," said the Governor, "and thank Allah that it is to a noble and a great man who would make no unworthy use of it that you have delivered a document testifying that Mohammed is an impostor. In future, venture not to enter into judgment with men whom it has pleased God to give more wit than to yourselves."

PARADISE SOLD BY THE YARD

The chief Imam of the Vilayet of Broussa owed to a Jew money-lender the sum of two hundred piasters. The Jew wanted his money and would give no rest to the Imam. Daily he came to ask for it, but without success. The Jew was becoming very anxious and determined to make a great effort. Not being able to take the Imam to court, he decided to try and shame him into paying the sum due; and to effect this, he came, sat on his debtor's doorstep and bewailed his sad fate in having fallen into the hands of a tyrant. The Imam saw that if this continued, his reputation as a man of justice would be considerably impaired, so he thought of a plan by which to pay off his creditor. Calling the Jew into his house, he said:

"Friend, what wilt thou do with the money if I pay thee?"

"Get food, clothe my children, and advance in my business," answered the Jew.

"My friend," said the Imam, "thy pitiful position awakens my compassion. Thou art gathering wealth in this world at the cost of thy soul and peace in the world to come; and I wish I could help thee. I will tell thee what I will do for thee. I would not do the same thing for any other Jew in the world, but thou hast awakened my commiseration. For the debt I owe thee, I will sell thee two hundred yards of Paradise, and being owner of this incomparable possession in the world to come, thou canst fearlessly go forth and earn as much as possible in this world, having already made ample provision for the next."

What could the Jew do but take what the Imam was willing to give him? So he accepted the deed for the two hundred yards of Paradise. A happy thought now struck the Jew. He set off and found the tithe-collector of the revenues of the mosque, and made friends with him. He then explained to him, when the intimacy had developed, how he was the possessor of a deed entitling him to two hundred yards of Paradise, and offered the collector a handsome commission if he would help him in disposing of it. When the money had been gathered for the quarter, the collector came and discounted the Imam's document, returning it to him as two hundred piasters of the tithes collected, with the statement that this document had been given to him by a peasant, and that bearing his holy seal, he dared not refuse it.

The Imam was completely deceived, and thought that the Jew had sold the deed at a discount to some of his subjects who were in arrears, and of course had to receive it as being as good as gold. Nevertheless the Jew was not forgotten, and the Imam determined to have him taken into court and sentenced if possible. His charge against the Jew was that he, the chief priest of the province, had taken pity on this Jew, thinking what a terrible thing it was to know no future, and as the man hitherto had an irreproachable character, in consideration of a small debt he had against the church, which it was desirable to balance, he thought he would give this Jew two hundred yards of Paradise, which he did.

"Now, gentlemen, this ungrateful dog sold this valuable document, and it was brought back to me as payment of taxes in arrears due to the church. Therefore, I say that this Jew has committed a great sin and ought to be punished accordingly."

The Cadis now turned to hear the Jew, who, the personification of meekness, stood as if awaiting his death sentence. With the most innocent look possible, the Jew replied, when the Cadis asked him what he had to say for himself:

"Effendim, it is needless to say how I appreciate the kindness of our Imam, but the reason that I disposed of that valuable document was this: When I went to Paradise I found a seat, and measured out my two hundred yards, and took possession of the further inside end of the bench. I had not been there long when a Turk came and sat beside me. I showed him my document and protested against his taking part of my seat; but, gentlemen, I assure you it was altogether useless; the Turks came and came, one after the other, till, to make a long story short, I fell off at the other end of the seat, and here I am. The Turks in Paradise will take no heed of your document, and either will not recognize the authority of the Imam, or will not let the Jews enter therein.

"Effendim, what could I do but come back and sell the document to men who could enter Paradise, and this I did."

The Cadis, after consulting, gave judgment as follows:

"We note that you could not have done anything else but sell the two hundred yards of Paradise, and the fact that you cannot enter there is ample punishment for the wrong committed; but there is still a grievous charge against you, which, if you can clear to our satisfaction, you will at once be dismissed. How much did the document cost you and what did you sell it for?"

"Effendim, it cost me two hundred piasters,

and I sold it for two hundred piasters."

This statement having been proved by producing the deed in question, and the tithe-collector who had given it to the Imam for two hundred piasters, the Jew was acquitted.

JEW TURNED TURK

irkedji, the landing-place on the Stamboul side of the Golden Horn, is always a scene of bustle and noise. The Caiquedjis, striving for custom, cry at the top of their voices: "I am bound for Haskeuy; I can take another man; my fare is a piaster!"

Others call in lusty tones, that they are bound for Karakeuy. Further out in the stream are other caiques, bound for more distant places, some with a passenger or two, others without. In one of these sat a Jew patiently waiting, while the Caiquedji, standing erect, backed in and out, every now and then calling at the top of his voice: 'Iuskidar,' meaning that he was bound for Scutari, on the Asiatic shore.

At last a Mussulman signed to him to approach, and inquired his fare. After some bargaining, the Turk entered the caique, and the boatman still held on to the pier in the hope of securing a third passenger, which, after a very short time, he did. The third passenger happened to be a Jew, who had forsaken his faith for that of Islam.

This converted individual saw at a glance that one of his fellow-passengers was a Moslem and the other a Jew, and wishing to gain favor in the eyes of the former, he called the other a 'Yahoudi' (meaning Jew, but usually employed as a term of disdain) and told him to make room for him. This the Jew meekly did, without a murmur, and the Caiquedji bent his oars for the Asiatic shore. The converted Jew and the Turk started a conversation, which they kept up till within a short distance of Scutari, when the Turk turned and said to the Jew, who had humbly been sitting on the low seat with bowed head and closed eyes:

"And what have you to say on the subject, Moses?"

"Alas! Pasha Effendi," answered the Jew, "I have been asleep, and have not followed your conversation; and if I had, what worth could my opinion be, I, a poor Jew?"

The converted Jew then said: "At least, you can tell us, to pass the time, where you have been in your sleep?" and he burst out laughing, thinking it a capital joke.

"I dreamt I was in Paradise," replied the poor Jew. "Oh! it was wonderful! There were three great golden gates, and on the inside, at the side of the keeper of each gate, stood Mohammed at one, Moses at the other, and Jesus at the third. No one was allowed to pass into Paradise, unless Mohammed, Moses, or Jesus gave the order that they should pass. At Mohammed's gate a man knocked, and on being opened, the keeper asked:

"'What is your name?' to which he replied, 'Ahmet.'

"'And your father's name?' again asked the keeper. 'Abdullah.'

"And the prophet signed with his hand that he might enter.

"I then went to the gate where Jesus stood, and heard the same questions put to an applicant. He told the keeper that his name was Aristide, and that his father's name was Vassili, and Jesus permitted him to enter.

"Hearing a loud knocking at Mohammed's gate

again, I hurried to see who the important comer was. There stood a man of confident mien, who proudly answered that his name was Hussein Effendi.

"'And your father's name?' asked the keeper. 'Abraham,' replied Hussein. At this Mohammed said: 'Shut the door; you can't enter here; mixtures will not do.'"

"Eh! What happened next?" asked the Turk.

"Just then, as the gate was shutting, I heard your voice and I awoke, Pasha Effendi," answered the Jew; "and so I can't tell you."

And as they approached the Scala (landing), they disembarked at Scutari and separated without a word.

THE METAMORPHOSIS

ussein Agha was much troubled in spirit and mind. He had saved a large sum of money in order that he might make the pilgrimage to Mecca. What troubled him was, that after having carefully provided for all the expenses of this long journey there still remained a few hundred piasters over and above. What was he to do with these? True, they could be distributed amongst the poor, but then, might not he, on his return, require the money for even a more meritorious purpose?

After much consideration, he decided that it was not Allah's wish that he should at once give this money in charity. On the other hand, he felt convinced that he should not give it to a brother for safe keeping, as he might be inspired, during Hussein's pilgrimage, to spend it on some charitable purpose. After a time he thought of a kindly Jew who was his neighbor, and decided to leave his savings in the hands of this man, to whom Allah had been good, seeing that his possessions were great. After mature thought he decided not to put temptation in the way of his neighbor. He therefore secured a jar, at the bottom of which he placed a small bag containing his surplus of wealth, and filled it with olives. This he carried to his neighbor, and begged him to take care of it for him. Ben Moïse of course consented, and Hussein Agha departed on his pilgrimage, contented.

On his return from the Holy Land, Hussein, now a Hadji, repaired to Ben Moïse and asked for his jar of olives, and at the same time presented Ben Moïse with a rosary of Yemen stones, in recognition of the service rendered him in the safe keeping of the olives, which, he said, were exceptionally palatable. Ben Moïse thanked him, and Hadji Hussein departed with his jar, well satisfied.

During the absence of Hussein Agha, it happened that Ben Moïse had some distinguished visitors, to whom, as is the Eastern custom, he served raki. Unfortunately, however, he had no mézé (appetizer) to offer, as is also the custom in the East. Ben Moïse bethought him of the olives and immediately went to the cellar, opened the jar, and extracted some of them, saying: "Olives are not rare; Hussein will never know the difference if I replace them."

The olives were found excellent, and Ben Moïse again and again helped his friends to them. Great was his surprise when he found that instead of olives, he brought forth a bag containing a quantity of gold. Ben Moïse could not understand this phenomenon, but appropriated the gold and held his peace.

Arriving home, poor Hussein Agha was distracted to find that his jar contained nothing but olives. Vainly did he protest to Ben Moïse.

"My friend," he would reply, "you gave me the jar, saying it contained olives. I believed you and kept the jar safe for you. Now you say that in the jar you had put some money together with the olives; perhaps you did, but is not that the jar you gave me? If, as you say, there was gold in the jar and it is now gone, all I can say is, the stronger has overcome the weaker, and that in this case the gold has either been converted into olives or into oil. What can I do? The jar you gave me I returned to you."

Hadji Hussein admitted this, and fully appreciated that he had no case against the Jew, so saying: 'Chok shai!' he returned to his home.

That night Hussein mingled in his prayers a vow to recover his gold at no matter what cost or trouble.

In his younger days Hadji Hussein had been a pipe-maker, and many were the chibooks of exceptional beauty that he had made. Go but to the potters' lane at Tophane, and the works of art displayed by the majority of them have been fashioned by the hands of Hussein. The art that had fed him for years was now to be the means of recovering his money.

Hadji Hussein daily met Ben Moïse but he never again referred to the money, and further, Hussein's sons were always in company with Ben Moïse's only son, a lad of ten.

Time passed, and Ben Moïse entirely forgot about the jar, olives, and gold; not so Hadji Hussein. He had been working. First he had made an effigy of Ben Moïse. When he had completed this image to his satisfaction, he dressed it in the identical manner and costume the Jew habitually wore. He then purchased a monkey. This monkey was kept in a cage opposite the effigy of Ben Moïse. Twice a day regularly the monkey's food was placed on the shoulders of the Jew, and Hussein would open the cage, saying: "Babai git" (go to your father). At a bound the monkey would plant himself on the shoulders of the Jew, and would not be dislodged until its hunger had been satisfied.

In the meantime Hadji Hussein and Ben Moïse were greater friends than ever, and their children were likewise playmates. One day Hussein took Ben

Moïse's son to his Harem and told him, much to the lad's joy, that he was to be their guest for a week. Later on Ben Moïse called on Hadji Hussein to know the reason of his son's not returning as usual at sundown.

"Ah, my friend," said Hussein, "a great calamity has befallen you! Your son, alas! has been converted into a monkey, a furious monkey! So furious that I was compelled to put him into a cage. Come and see for yourself."

No sooner did Ben Moïse enter the room in which the caged monkey was, than it set up a howl, not having had any food that day. Poor Ben Moïse was thunderstruck, and Hadji Hussein begged him to take the monkey away.

Next day Hussein was summoned to the court, the case of Ben Moïse was heard, and the Hadji was ordered to return the child at once. This he vowed he could not do, and to convince the judges he offered to bring the monkey caged as it was to the court, and, Inshallah, they would see for themselves that the child of the Jew had been converted into a monkey. This was ultimately agreed to, and the monkey was brought. Hadji Hussein took special care to place the cage opposite Ben Moïse, and no sooner did the monkey catch sight of him than it set up a scream, and the judges said: 'Chok shai!' Hussein Agha then opened the cage door, saying: "Go to your father," and the monkey with a bound and a yell embraced Ben Moïse, putting his head, in search of food, first on one shoulder of the Jew and then on the other. The judges were thunderstruck, and declared their incompetency to give judgment in such a case. Ben Moïse protested, saying that it was against the laws of nature for such a metamorphosis to take place, whereupon Hadji Hussein told the judges of an analogous instance of some gold pieces turning into olives, and called upon Ben Moïse to witness the veracity of his statement. The judges, much perplexed, dismissed the case, declaring that provision had not been made in the law for it, and there being no precedent to their knowledge they were incompetent to give judgment.

Leaving the court, Hadji Hussein informed Ben Moïse that there would still be pleasure and happiness in this world for him, provided he could reconvert the olives into gold. Needless to add that Ben Moïse handed the money to Hadji Hussein, and the heir of Ben Moïse returned to his home none the worse for his transformation.

THE CALIF OMAR

The Calif Omar, one of the first Califs after the Prophet, is deeply venerated to this day, and is continually quoted as a lover of truth and justice. Often in the face of appalling evidence he refrained from judgment, thus liberating the innocent and punishing the guilty. The following is given as an example of his perseverance in fathoming a murder.

At the feast of the Passover, a certain Jew of Bagdad had sacrificed his sheep and was offering up his prayers, when suddenly a dog came in, and snatching up the sheep's head ran off with it. The Jew pursued in hot haste, in his excitement still carrying the bloody knife and wearing his besmeared apron. The dog, carrying the sheep's head, rushed into an open doorway, followed closely by the Jew. The Jew in his hurried pursuit fell over the body of what proved to be a murdered man. The murder was laid against the Jew, and witnesses swore that they had seen him coming out of the house covered with blood, and in his hand a bloody dagger. The Jew was arrested and tried, but with covered head he swore by his forefathers and children that he was innocent. Omar would not condemn him as none of the witnesses had seen the Jew do the deed, and until further evidence had been given to prove his guilt the case was adjourned. Spies and detectives, unknown to anybody, were put to track the murderers. After a time they were discovered, condemned, put to death, and the Jew liberated.

KALAIDJI AVRAM OF BALATA

Balata, situated on the Golden Horn, is mostly inhabited by Jews of the poorer classes, who make their livelihood as tinsmiths, tinkers, and hawkers.

Here, in the early days when the Janissaries flourished, there lived a certain tinsmith called Kalaidji Avram. Having rather an extensive business, his neighbors, especially those who lived nearest, were always complaining of the annoying smoke and disagreeable odor of ammonia which he used in tinning his pots and pans.

Opposite Avram's place the village guardhouse was situated, and the chief, a Janissary, often had disputes with Avram about the smoke. Avram would invariably reply: "I have my children to feed and I must work; and without smoke I cannot earn their daily bread."

The Janissary, much annoyed, cultivated a dislike for Avram and a thirst for revenge.

It happened that a Jew one day came to the Janissary and said to him: "Do you want to make a fortune? if so, you have the means of doing this, provided you will agree to halve with me whatever is made."

The Janissary, on being assured that he had but to say a word or two to a person he would designate and the money would be forthcoming, accepted the conditions. The Jew then said: "All you have to do is to go up to a Jewish funeral procession that will pass by here to-morrow on its way to the necropolis outside the city, and order it to stop. It is against the religion of the Jews for such a thing to happen, and the Chacham (rabbi) will offer you first ten, then twenty, and finally one hundred and ten thousand piasters to allow the funeral to proceed. The half will be for you to compensate you for your trouble and the other fifty-five thousand piasters for me."

This, as the Jew had told him, seemed very simple to the Janissary. The next day, true enough, he beheld a funeral, and immediately went out and ordered it to stop. The Chacham protested, offering first small bribes, then larger and larger, till ultimately he promised to bring to the worthy captain one hundred and ten thousand piasters for allowing the funeral to proceed.

That evening, as agreed, the Chacham came and handed the money to the captain of the Janissaries. Then taking another bag containing a second one hundred and ten thousand piasters, he said: "If you will tell me who informed you that we would pay so much money rather than have a funeral stopped, you can have this further sum."

The Janissary immediately bethought him of Avram, the tinsmith, and accused him as his informant, and the Chacham, satisfied, paid the sum and departed.

Avram disappeared nobody knew where. The Chacham said that death had taken him for his own as a punishment for stopping him while on a journey.

The accomplice of the Janissary came a few days later for his share of the money. The Janissary handed him the fifty-five thousand piasters, and at the same time said: "Of these fifty-five thousand piasters, thirty thousand must be given to the widow and children of Avram, and I advise you to give it willingly, for Avram has taken your place."

.

HOW MEHMET ALI PASHA OF EGYPT ADMINISTERED JUSTICE

Jewish merchant was in the habit of borrowing, and sometimes of lending money to an Armenian merchant of Cairo. Receipts were never exchanged, but at the closing of an old account or the opening of a new one they would simply say to each other, I have debited or credited you in my books, as the case might be, with so much.

On one occasion the Armenian lent the Jew the sum of twenty-five thousand piasters, and after the usual verbal acknowledgment the Armenian made his entry. A reasonable time having elapsed, the Armenian sent his greetings to the Jew. This, in Eastern etiquette, meant, 'Kindly pay me what you owe.' The Jew, however, did not take the hint but returned complimentary greetings to the Armenian. This was repeated several times. Finally, the Armenian sent a message requesting the Jew to call upon him. The Jew, however, told the messenger to inform the Armenian merchant, that if he wished to see him, he must come to his house. The Armenian called upon the Jew, and requested payment of the loan. The Jew brought out his books and showed the Armenian that he was both credited and debited with the sum of twenty-five thousand piasters. The Armenian protested, but in vain; the Jew maintained that the debt had been paid.

In the hope of recovering his money, the Armenian had the case brought before Mehmet Ali Pasha of Egypt, a clever and learned judge. No witnesses, however, could be cited to prove that the money had either been borrowed or repaid. The entries were verified, and it was thought that perhaps the Armenian had forgotten. Before dismissing the case, however, Mehmet Ali Pasha called in the Public Weigher and ordered that both the Armenian and Jewish merchants be weighed. This done, Mehmet Ali Pasha took note of their respective weights. The Jew weighed fifty okes and the Armenian sixty okes. He then discharged them, saying that he would send for them later on.

The Armenian waited patiently for a month or two, but no summons came from the Pasha. Every Friday he endeavored to meet the Pasha so as to bring the case to his mind, but without avail; for the Pasha, perceiving him from a distance, would turn away his head or otherwise purposely avoid catching his eye. At last, after about eight months of anxious waiting, the Armenian and the Jew were summoned to appear before the court. Mehmet Ali Pasha, in opening the case, called in the Public Weigher and had them weighed again. On this occasion it was found that the Armenian had decreased, now only weighing fifty okes, for worry makes a man grow thin; but the Jew, on the contrary, had put on several okes. These facts were gravely considered, and the Pasha accused the Jew of having received the money and at once ordered the brass pot to be heated and placed on his head to force confession. The Jew did not care to submit to this fearful ordeal, so he confessed that he had not repaid the debt, and had to do so then and there.

HOW THE FARMER LEARNED TO CURE HIS WIFE — A TURKISH ÆSOP

here once lived a farmer who understood the language of animals. He had obtained this knowledge on condition that he would never reveal its possession, and with the further provision that should he prove false to his oath the penalty would be certain death.

One day he chanced to listen to a conversation his ox and his horse were having. The ox had just come in from a weary and hard day's work in the rain.

"Oh," sighed the ox, looking over to the horse, "how fortunate you are to have been born a horse and not an ox. When the weather is bad you are kept in the stable, well fed, groomed every morning, and caressed every evening. Oh that I were a horse!"

"What you say is true," replied the horse, "but you are very stupid to work so hard."

"You do not know what it is to be goaded with a spear and howled at, or you would not accuse me of being stupid to work so hard," replied the ox.

"Then why don't you feign sickness," continued the horse.

On the following day the ox determined to try this deceit, but he was stung with remorse when he saw the horse led out to take his place at the plough. In the evening, when the horse was brought to the stable very tired, the ox sympathized with him, and regretted his being the cause, but at the same time expressed astonishment at his working so hard.

"Ah, my friend, I had to work hard; I can't bear the whip; the thought of the hideous crack! crack! makes me shiver even now," answered the horse.

"But leaving that aside, my poor horned friend," proceeded the horse, "I am now most anxious for you. I heard the master say to-night that if you were not well in the morning, the butcher was to come and slaughter you."

"You need not worry about me, friend horse," said the ox, "as I much prefer the yoke to chewing the cud of self-reproach."

At this point the farmer left the animals and entered his home, smiling at his own wily craft in re-establishing, if not contentedness, at least resignation to their fate, in the stable. Meeting his wife, she at once inquired as to the cause of his happy smile. He put her off, first with one excuse then with another, but to no avail; the more he protested, the stronger her inquisitiveness grew. Her unsatisfied curiosity at length made her ill. The endeavors of the numerous doctors brought to her assistance were as futile as the incantations of the sages from far and near, and as powerless to remove the spell as were the amulets, the charms, and the abracadabras conceived and written by holy men. The evil prompting gnawed her, and she visibly pined away. The poor farmer was distracted. Rather than see her die, he at last decided to tell her, and forfeit his own life to save hers. Deeply dejected, for no man quits this planet without a pang, he sat at the window gazing, as he thought, for the last time on the familiar surroundings. Of a sudden he noticed his favorite chanticleer, followed by his numerous harem, sadly strutting about, only allowing his favorites to eat the morsels he discovered, and ruthlessly driving the others away. To one he said: "I am not like our poor master, to be ruled by one or a score of you. He, poor man, will die to-day for revealing his secret knowledge to save her life."

"What is the secret knowledge?" asked one of the wives; and the chanticleer flew at her and thrashed her mercilessly, saying at each vigorous blow, "That is the secret, and if our master only treated the mistress as I treat you, he would not need to give up his life to-day."

And as if maddened at the thought, he beat them all in turn. The master, seeing and appreciating the effect from the window, went to his wife and treated her in precisely the same manner. And this effected what neither doctors, sages, nor holy men could do — it cured her.

THE LANGUAGE OF BIRDS

here once lived a Hodja who, it was said, understood the language of birds, but refused to impart his knowledge. One young man was very persistent in his desire to know the language of these sweet creatures, but the Hodja was inflexible.

In despair, the young man went to the woods at least to listen to the pleasant chirping of the birds. By degrees it conveyed to him a meaning, till, finally, he understood them to tell him that his horse would die. On returning from the woods, he immediately sold his horse and went and told the Hodja.

"Oh Hodja, why will you not teach me the language of birds? Yesterday I went to the woods and they warned me that my horse would die, thus affording me an opportunity of selling it and avoiding the loss."

The Hodja was silent, but would not give way.

The following day the young man again went to the woods, and the chirping of the birds told him that his house would be burned. The young man hurried away, sold his house, again went to the Hodja and told him all that had happened, adding:

"See, Hodja Effendi, you would not teach me the language of the birds, but I have saved my horse and my house by listening to them."

On the following day, the young man again went to the woods, and the birds chirped him the doleful tale, that on the following day he would die. In tears the young man went to the Hodja for advice.

"Oh Hodja Effendi! Alas! What am I to do? The birds have told me that to-morrow I must die."

"My son," answered the Hodja, "I knew this would come, and that is why I refused to teach you the language of birds. Had you borne the loss of your horse, your house would have been saved, and had your house been burned, your life would have been saved."

THE SWALLOW'S ADVICE

A man one day saw a swallow and caught it. The bird pleaded hard for liberty, saying:

"If thou wilt let me go, thy gain will be great, for I will give thee three counsels that will hereafter be of use to thee."

The man listened to the bird and let it go. Flying to a tree close by it perched on a branch, and said:

"Hearken and give thine ear to the three advices that will guide thee. The first is, do not believe things that are incredible; the second is, do not attempt to stretch out thine hand to a place thou art unable to reach; and the third advice I give thee is, do not pine after a thing that is past and gone. Take these my counsels and do not forget them."

The bird then tempted the man, saying: "Inside of me there is a large pearl of great value; it is both magnificent and splendid, and as large as the egg of a kite."

Now, hearing this, the man repented at having let the bird go, the color of his face went to sadness, and he at once stretched out his hand to catch the swallow, but the latter said to the foolish man:

"What! Hast thou already forgotten the advice I gave thee, and the lie which I told thee, hast thou considered as true? I had fallen into thy hands, yet thou wert unable to retain me, and now thou art sorrowing for the past for which there is no remedy."

Such are those that worship idols, and give the

name of God to their own handiwork. They have left aside God Almighty, and have forgotten the Great Bestower of all good gifts.

WE KNOW NOT WHAT THE DAWN
MAY BRING FORTH

n the age of the Janissaries the Minister of War, in all haste, called the chief farrier of the Army and ordered him to have made immediately two hundred thousand horseshoes. The farrier was aghast, and explained that to make such a quantity of horseshoes, both time and smiths would be required. The Minister replied:

"It is the order of his Majesty that these two hundred thousand horseshoes be ready by to-morrow; if not, your head will pay the penalty."

The poor farrier replied, that knowing now that he was doomed he would be unable, through nervousness, to make even a fifth of the number. The Minister would not listen to reason, and left in anger, reiterating the order of his Majesty.

The farrier retired to his rooms deeply dejected. His wife, woman-like, endeavored to encourage and comfort him, saying:

"Cheer up, husband, drink your raki, eat your mézé, and be cheerful, for we know not what the dawn may bring forth."

"Ah!" said the farrier, "the dawn will not bring forth two hundred thousand horseshoes, and my head will pay the penalty."

Late that night there was a tremendous knocking at his door. The poor farrier thought that it was an inquiry as to how many horseshoes were already made, and trembling with fear went and opened the door. What was his surprise, when on opening the door and inquiring the object of the visit, to be greeted with:

"Haste, farrier, let us have sixteen nails, for the Minister of War has been suddenly removed to Paradise by the hand of Allah."

The farrier gathered, not sixteen but forty nails of the best he had, and, handing them to the messenger, said:

"Nail him down well, friend, so that he will not get up again, for had not this happened, the nails would have been required to keep me in my coffin."

OLD MEN MADE YOUNG

n Psamatia, an ancient Armenian village situated near the Seven Towers, there lived a certain smith, whose custom it was, in contradiction to prescribed rules, to curse the devil and his works regularly five times a day instead of praying to God. He argued that it is the devil's fault that man had need to pray. The devil was angered at being thus persistently cursed, and decided to punish the smith, or at least prevent his causing further trouble.

Taking the form of a young man he went to the smith and engaged himself as an apprentice. After a time the devil told the smith that he had a very poor and mean way of earning a living, and that he would show him how money was to be made. The smith asked what he, a young apprentice, could do. Thereupon the devil told him that he was endowed with a great gift: the power to make old men young again. Though incredulous, after continued assurance the smith allowed a sign to be put above his door, stating that aged people could here be restored to youth. This extraordinary sign attracted a great many, but the devil asked such high prices that most went away, preferring age to parting with so much money.

At last one old man agreed to pay the sum demanded by the devil, whereupon he was promptly cast into the furnace, the master-smith blowing the bellows for a small remuneration. After a time of vigorous blowing the devil raked out a young man. The fame of the smith extended far and wide, and many were the aged that came to regain their youth. This lucrative business went on for some time, and at last the smith, thinking to himself that it was not a difficult thing to throw a man into the furnace and rake him out from the ashes restored to youth, decided to do away with his apprentice's services, but kept the sign above the door.

It happened that the captain of the Janissaries, who was a very aged man, came to him, and after bargaining for a much more modest sum than his apprentice would have asked, the smith thrust him into the furnace as the devil, his apprentice, used to do, and worked at the bellows. He afterwards raked in the fire for the young man but he only raked out cinders and ashes. Great was his consternation, but what could he do?

The devil in the meantime went to the head of the Janissaries and the police, and informed them of what had taken place. The poor smith was arrested, tried, and condemned to be bowstrung, as it was proved that the Janissary was last seen to enter his shop.

Just as the smith was about to be executed, the devil again appeared before him in the form of the discharged apprentice, and asked him if he wished to be saved; if so, that he could save him, but on one condition only, — that he ceased from cursing the devil five times a day and pray as other Mussulmans prayed. He agreed. Thereupon the apprentice called in a loud voice to those who were about to execute him: "What will you of this man? He has not killed the Janissary; he is not dead, for I have just seen him entering his home." This was found to be true, and the smith was liberated, learning the truth of the proverb, 'Curse not even the devil.'

THE BRIBE

There once lived in Stamboul a man and wife who were so well mated that though married for a number of years their life was one of ideal harmony. This troubled the devil very much. He had destroyed the peace of home after home; he had successfully created, between husband and wife, father and son and brothers, the chasm of envy wide and deep, so wide that the bridge of life could not span the gap. In this one little home alone did he fail in spite of his greatest endeavor. One day the devil was talking to an old woman, when the man who had thus far baffled him passed by. The devil groaned at the thought of his repeated failures. Turning to the old woman he said:

"I will give you as a reward a pair of yellow slippers if you make that man quarrel with his wife."

The old woman was delighted, and at once began to scheme and work for the coveted slippers. At an hour when she was sure to find the lady alone, she went and solicited alms, weeping and bemoaning her sad fate at being a lonely old woman whose husband was long since dead. She appealed to the lady for compassion in proportion as she hoped for the duration of the cup she and her husband quaffed in undivided happiness. The lady was very generous to the old woman, each day giving her something; so much so, that the thought that her good husband might think her extravagant often gave her some uneasiness.

One day the old woman looked into the shop-door of her benefactress's husband and planted the first evil seed by calling out:

"Ah! if men only knew where the money they work for from morning till night goes, or knew what their wives did when they were away, some homes would not be so happy."

The evil woman then went her way, and the good shopman wondered why she had said these words to him. A passing thought suggested that it was strange that of late his wife had asked him several times for a few extra piasters. The next day, the old woman as usual solicited alms of her victim. In the fulness of her hypocrisy she embraced the young lady before departing, taking care to leave the imprint of her blackened hand on her dupe's back. The old woman then again went to the shop, looked at her victim's husband, and said:

"Oh! how blind men are! They only look in a woman's face for truth and loyalty; they forget to look at the back where the stamp of the lover's hand is to be seen."

As before, the old woman disappeared. But the mind of the shopman was troubled and his heart was heavy. In this oppressed state he went to his home, and an opportunity offering he looked at his wife's back, and was aghast to see there the impression of a hand. He got up and left his home, a broken-hearted man.

The devil was deeply impressed at the signal success of the old woman, and hastened to redeem his promise. He took a long pole, tied the pair of slippers at the end, and hurried off to the old woman. Arriving at her house he called out to her to open the window. When she did this, he thrust in the pair of yellow slippers, begging her to take them, but not to come near him; they were hard-earned slippers, he said; she had succeeded where he had failed; so that he was afraid of her and was anxious to keep out of her way.

HOW THE DEVIL LOST HIS WAGER

A peasant, ploughing his field, was panting with fatigue, when the devil appeared before him and said:

"Oh, poor man! you complain of your lot, and with justice; for your labor is not that of a man, but is as heavy as that of a beast of burden. Now I have made a wager that I shall find a contented man; so give me the handle of your plough and the goad of your oxen, that I may do the work for you."

The peasant consenting, the devil touched the oxen and in one turn of the plough all the furrows of the field were opened up and the work finished.

"Is it well done?" asked the devil.

"Yes," replied the man, "but seed is very dear this year."

In answer to this, the devil shook his long tail in the air, and lo, little seeds began to fall like hail from the sky.

"I hope," said the devil, "that I have gained my wager."

"Bah," answered the peasant, "what's the good of that? These seeds might be lost. You do not take into consideration frost, blighting winds, drought, damp, storms, diseases of plants, and other things. How can I judge as yet?"

"Behold," said the devil, "in this box are both sun and rain, take it and use it as you please."

The peasant did so and to very good purpose, for his corn soon ripened and up to that time he had never seen so good a harvest. But the corn of his neighbors had also prospered from the rain and sun.

At harvest time the devil came, and saw that the man was looking with envious eyes at his neighbor's fields where the corn was as good as his own.

"Have you been able to obtain what you desired?" asked the devil.

"Alas!" answered the man, "all the barns will break down under the weight of the sheaves. The grain will be sold at a low price. This fine harvest will make me sit on ashes."

While he was speaking, the devil had taken an ear of corn from the ground and was crushing it in his hand, and as soon as he blew on the grains they all turned into pure gold. The peasant took up one and examined it attentively on all sides, and then in a despairing tone cried out: "Oh, my God! I must spend money to melt all these and send them to the mint."

The devil wrung his hands in despair. He had lost his wager. He could do everything, but he could not make a contented man.

THE EFFECTS OF RAKI

Bekri Mustafe, who lived during the reign of Sultan Selim, was a celebrated toper, and perhaps at that time the only Moslem drunkard in Turkey. Consequently, he was often the subject of conversation in circles both high and low. It happened that his Majesty the Sultan had occasion to speak to Bekri one day, and he asked him what pleasure he found in drinking so much raki, and why he disobeyed the laws of the Prophet. Bekri replied that raki was a boon to man; that it made the deaf to hear, the blind to see, the lame to walk, and the poor rich, and that he, Bekri, when drunk, could hear, see, and walk like two Bekris. The Sultan, to verify the truth of this statement, sent his servants into the highways to bring four men, the one blind, the other deaf, the third lame, and the fourth poor. Directly these were brought, his Majesty ordered raki to be served to them in company with Bekri. They had not been drinking long when, to the glory of Bekri, the deaf man said: "I hear the sound of great rumbling."

And the blind man replied: "I can see him; it is an enemy who seeks our destruction."

The lame man asked where he was, saying, "Show him to me, and I will quickly despatch him."

And the poor man called out: "Don't be afraid to kill him; I've got his blood money in my pocket."

Just then a funeral happened to pass by the Palace buildings, and Bekri got up and ordered the solemn procession to stop. Removing the lid of the coffin, he whispered a few words into the ear of the dead man, and then putting his ear to the dead man's mouth, vented an exclamation of surprise. He then ordered the funeral to proceed, and returned to the Palace.

The Sultan asked him what he had said to the dead man, and what the dead man replied.

"I simply asked him where he was going and from what he had died, and he replied he was going to Paradise, and that he had died from drinking raki without a mézé."

Whereupon the Sultan understanding what he wanted, ordered that the mézé should be immediately served.